My Name Was Never
FRANKENSTEIN

My Name Was Never FRANKENSTEIN

And Other Classic Adventure Tales Remixed

Edited by

BRYAN FURUNESS

INDIANA UNIVERSITY PRESS

This book is a publication of

INDIANA UNIVERSITY PRESS
Office of Scholarly Publishing
Herman B Wells Library 350
1320 East 10th Street
Bloomington, Indiana 47405 USA

iupress.indiana.edu

Manufactured in the United States of America

Library of Congress Cataloging-in-Publication Data

Names: Furuness, Bryan, editor, author.
Title: My name was never Frankenstein ; and other classic
    adventure tales remixed / edited by Bryan Furuness.
Other titles: Classic adventure tales remixed
Description: Bloomington, Indiana : Indiana University
    Press, [2018] | Identifiers: LCCN 2018019385 (print) |
    LCCN 2018025458 (ebook) | ISBN 9780253036360
    (e-book) | ISBN 9780253036346 (cl : alk. paper) |
    ISBN 9780253036353 (pb : alk. paper)
Subjects: LCSH: Fictitious characters—Fiction. | Short
    stories. | GSAFD: Adventure stories. | Suspense fiction.
Classification: LCC PN6120.95.A38 (ebook) | LCC PN6120.95
    .A38 M9 2018 (print) | DDC 808.83/87—dc23
LC record available at https://lccn.loc.gov/2018019385

1 2 3 4 5   23 22 21 20 19 18

For my boys, Eli and Evan:
You are my adventure.

Reprinted by Permission

CONTENTS

Acknowledgments

THE EDITOR WISHES TO THANK HIS EDITOR, ASHLEY RUNYON, WHO launched this whole adventure. Thank you, too, to the whole team at Break Away Books and Indiana University Press. An honor and a pleasure to work with you.

Thank you to *Booth* and its editor in chief, Rob Stapleton, for the logistical and moral support. Always good to run with you, Chief.

The last and biggest goes to my family. None of this would be possible without you. Us, always.

INTRODUCTION

AT THE BEGINNING OF *THE MAGICIAN KING* BY LEV GROSSMAN, THE main character—Quentin—is a king in the land of Fillory. He's a magician in a magical land, but he's grown a little bored of the whole scene. Then one day the royal court comes upon an ancient clock tree thrashing in a wind that no one else can feel. "It was a Fillorian wonder, a real one, wild and grand and strange," and Quentin feels "a twinge of . . . fear, and something more. Awe. They were looking the mystery in the face. This was the raw stuff, the main line, the old, old magic."

As you might predict, Quentin is drawn toward the clock tree, and an adventure begins.

In our world, stories are old magic. Some stories are more raw and elemental than others, though. Some fictional universes are wild frontiers, begging for exploration. Myths, for example. Fairy tales. And the newer territory of adventure tales.

Consider Tarzan. Zorro. Ahab. Nemo. You know them, even if you have never read the books or seen the movies. They're embedded in the cloud of our culture, our network of subconscious minds. Classic adventure tales are our new myths (though old enough, fortunately for this project, to be in the public domain). The characters from adventure tales are endlessly fascinating, their universes expansive. Like Quentin, I'm drawn toward this magic.

Fortunately, I'm not alone. Plenty of writers want to play with this magic, too. All the stories in this book use a classic adventure tale as a jumping-off point, but they jump in different directions. You'll see prequels, alternate universes, spin-offs, and total reboots. The result is an eclectic mix of tales, some wry, some haunting, but all captivating. It's wild and grand and strange, so let's get to it. And, who knows, maybe in the end you'll want to enter these mysteries and play with this magic, too.

My Name Was Never

FRANKENSTEIN

1

THE RETURN OF THE APE MAN

Edward Porter

Cheeta

I haven't seen Jane in years. Last I heard she had an antiques shop in Pasadena. I couldn't face her. I don't want her to see the way I am now. My pelt looks like Methuselah's bath mat. I barely have any paunch left, and I used to have a nice fat one, too. I can't remember the last time I had a good grooming. These days, I'm lucky if I remember to check my own head for ticks. One day you're an alpha and you think it'll last forever, then you're a beta, then . . . I don't know, the bottom drops out, and you're way downstream in the white man alphabet. Not that I give a damn. Don't have a troop, don't want one; been there, swung on that, thank you very much.

In LA, nobody wants to hear your shitty little story anyway. Gomangani, Tarmangani, my aunt Fanny, no one cares, just pay your tab. And I didn't blow my movie money, not all of it. My PETA rep got me disability, too. I should have been dead forever ago. I'm going to sit here by the hotel pool with my Hennessey and my Dunhills until the janitor puts me in the compost bin. I want to go out like Warren Zevon. Look away down Gower Avenue, know what I'm saying?

Him? You mean, His Lordship? No idea where he is. Don't know, don't care. I won't say his jungle name. I won't give him that anymore. He's forfeited the moral right to it, as far as I'm concerned. Did you know he trademarked it, and he'll sue your ass if you use it? I call it the T-word. If I have to talk about him, I call him that, or His Lordship. It's funny, nobody remembers his actual name. It's John. How boring is that? Me John—you Jane. What a farce.

I believed in him once. It seems ludicrous now. All I can say is, you didn't know him when. He was beautiful, man. Once.

What did I see in her? I know what you're thinking. You bet I just wanted to fuck the boss's girlfriend. Or maybe you think it was revenge for the way I came off in the movies, like I was his errand boy. "Cheeta! Run for help! Get Tantor the elephant!" Every time the action heated up, and the kids stopped fighting over jujubes and actually watched the movie, all you'd see of me is my scrawny naked ass hustling off screen. Then you wouldn't see me again until just before the credits, when I'd be in the background hitting myself in the head with a palm leaf as the music came up. You know what the business was like back then. They didn't want it good, they wanted it Thursday. But I have no regrets, and I think my work stands up. I did what I could with the writing I was given. Anyway, that was years later. So no, it wasn't about payback. I fell for her hard.

I can't say she was a looker. Body like a snake with breasts, weird green eyes, no fur, that bizarre, grub-colored skin. Nothing much in the way of nails, nothing that could really dig into a guy's fur and come up with the lice. And, oh my fucking Christ, that leopard-skin one-piece. I still get the heebie-jeebies thinking about it. It made her look sad and lost, like she was pretending to be something she wasn't. That wasn't her idea. He put her in that outfit. He wanted everyone to know she belonged to him. How messed up is that, to dress your girlfriend like she's a little you?

I can't tell you the number of times the two of them showed up at the clearing and the whole troop looked at each other, like, can you believe this? Are they for real? I mean, I'm a chimpanzee, and you're dressing as a leopard. Do you have any idea how disturbing that is for me? It's an insult, if you want to know the truth. What if my kid sees you? He's going to have a conniption. But that's not the worst of it. After he settles down and gets used to you, after you two play with him, bounce him around, put him on your weird, hairless shoulders, is he going to lose his fear of leopards? Because that is a big problem right there. I am definitely not okay with my kid thinking leopards are cool. For that matter, the name he gave me: Cheeta. Cheetahs are one of my predators, too. What if I got to name him Cancer or Polio? Why did he have to give me a new name in the first place? What the hell is wrong with Harold?

But they were careless people, he and Jane. They smashed up things and creatures—like wildebeests and hippos—then retreated back into their tools and anthropocentrism, or whatever else it was that kept them together, and left the rest of us to pick up the doo-doo they left on the forest floor.

So what did I see in her? She saw *me*. She saw the simian and accepted it for what it was, but she also saw a sensitive, curious guy with an inner world like her own.

His Lordship was just a blur of motion. Run! Swim! Climb! Find the poachers! Wrestle the crocodile! Fight the lion! Just vine to jolly old vine all day long. I admit, I admired his moxie. He never chickened out on anyone, never said, "I'm tired, let Alan Quartermain deal with Queen La today." There was something pure about him, back in the jungle. He was hardly enlightened. He'd stab anything or anybody and not think twice. He took killing guys from Mbonga's tribe about as seriously as badminton. But we were all like that, back then. I used to have quite the yen for monkey liver. You want to say I ate my relatives, knock yourself out. My point is, he had clear ideas about right and wrong—however grotesque— and he always acted on them. But all he did was act, and that gets exhausting. How can you get close to someone who never stops moving? How do you get quality time with someone who's always hanging from a cliff?

Jane was different. One time His Lordship was off climbing to the top of the waterfall to see which way the kaiser's secret battalion of gold robbers had gone, and she and I had fifteen minutes to ourselves. We were on that beautiful ridgeline on the west side of Kilimanjaro, just past the gorge. There's a stretch of gently sloping pink basalt that you can lean back on like a Barcalounger, and we sat taking the evening air, looking at Venus come up out of the sunset, the sky pink and gold and shimmering, like a baby mamba's first set of scales, with the black-green jungle below us, and that rooty, gingery baobab smell rising up and mingling with the jasmine and the kola nut flower. It got to me, and I blew out hard through my nostrils, the way you do when it's all so much no pant-hoot or hoot-grunt can even begin to express your yearning. She reached out, ran her hand over my occipital bump, and said, "Oh, Cheeta, I know. I feel it, too."

We were interspecies before it was trendy. Back when it cost you. I remember one time the three of us were in a bar in Mombasa, after she'd broken up with him and started seeing me. He'd mostly gotten over it by then, or said he had. He was all about noble. He was going to be noble if it killed him.

"Let best primate win," he'd said when I told him I was in love with her, grinning like he had nothing to worry about. A week later, after she'd made her choice, he came by my tree in the morning, eyes red, lower lip trembling, and said, "T-word not have hard feelings. Cheeta and T-word still bros." He looked up at my leafy bower, obviously wondering if she was there right now, blissed out on afterglow, stretching her arms, arching her back, thinking about seconds. As it happened, that's exactly where she was and what she was doing, but I wasn't going to throw it in his face. "T-word wish you and Jane all happiness," he stammered, like it was his big gift, and went off into the bush, probably to stab something helpless. Noble, right?

Anyway, a few weeks later, the three of us were in the bar drinking warm beer because don't get me started on the Brits, and this fat Belgian poacher wearing a necklace of warthog tusks saw me and Jane holding hands and said to her, "Do you need a notepad?" I looked at him like, what's this guy's problem? He came a little closer. "I said, do you need a notepad, miss?" He could barely hold in the giggles.

"No," Jane said. "I don't think so. Why do you ask?" She was like that. A little too good-hearted, never had her eyes peeled for quicksand.

"Because you've already got the pencil!" he said, and cracked up, and the rest of the bar cracked up with him. And it hit me—he meant my penis.

Jane turned red. "Excuse me," she said, and headed for the ladies. I turned and looked over at His Lordship, and he was smirking.

"Why didn't you say something?" I asked, trying not to bare my canines. "Why do you think that's an okay conversation for someone to have with your best friends?"

"Cheeta too sensitive," he said. "Not everything about species."

I didn't even threat-display. I just swatted him off his barstool like he was a slug on my banana leaf. I may have weighed ninety pounds, but I was still a fucking chimpanzee and twice as strong as any man.

Then I turned on that fat Belgian fuck and showed him the canines, the incisors, the molars, the whole shebang, and he put his hands up, like, hey, whoa, he didn't want any trouble. He wasn't giggling now.

The Brit bartender said, in his constipated, plummy, Brit accent, "Perhaps you and your peculiar companion might leave us now." Talking to His Lordship, you understand. I turned back around and said, "Have the fucking courtesy—" I didn't finish the sentence. I just let it hang there.

Jane came out of the ladies and saw John Clayton, Lord Greystoke sitting on his lordly ass in the sawdust and groundnut shells, looking like driver ants just crawled up his butt. "Go outside," I told her. "You don't want to watch this, trust me."

"They're not worth it," she said.

"I agree," I said. "But you are."

She rolled her eyes and said, "Males!" For a second, I thought she was going to grab me under the arms, go ups-a-daisy, and carry me out. But then she looked right at me and saw I needed this. Like I said. She saw *me*. She bent down, kissed me on the lips, long, slow, and juicy, and I heard a little moan from the floor. "I love you," she said. "Don't be long." Then she walked out the door.

His Lordship curled his lip at me. I faced him, the bartender, the Belgian, and the rest of those *Homo sapiens* jungle cutters, all of them scared and waiting for me to make my move.

What did I do? I'm not going to lie. I took a dump right on the bar. It felt great, too. Best dump I ever took.

Later, I forgave the bastard. He left cigarettes and whiskey out on the veranda for a few nights, and I decided to call that an apology. I knew we'd all be dead of old age waiting for him to verbalize it.

Of course, once Jane and I got to Hollywood, they bent the rules for us. If you're a star, you get away with anything there. They looked the other way for Lassie and Timmy, too. At least we were both adults.

Life was great. We'd all made the big time. What could possibly go wrong?

She wanted a baby. I'd had something between four and eight of them myself, as far as I knew. Twelve, tops. But I was willing to do it again. After all, she'd be the one who'd be carrying it on her back for three years, not me. I pictured a little humanzee, part her and part me. I figured with her brains and my body the kid could go to UCLA on a gymnastics scholarship. So we tried for years. It's theoretically possible. It's closer than horses and donkeys. But it didn't happen. Maybe we felt too much pressure.

So one morning at the Malibu cottage over eggs Benedict, she said, "Let's adopt."

I said, "Great. We can drive down to San Diego tomorrow, pick one out at the zoo, and be back in time for that sunset sail to Catalina with Gable and Lombard. The kid can climb the rigging, get some sea air. It'll be a hoot, as long as he doesn't fall in the drink."

She smiled, reached past the jam to hold my paw, and said, "Guess again."

That knocked me for a loop, and I had to confront a hard truth. Jane aside, I didn't trust humans. Some kid I'd never met—I don't know. What if, instead of a father, he sees me as a pet? You feed a child, put a roof over its head, and then one day you're on a leash at someone's sweet sixteen party and they're calling you Mr. Pebbles. I felt vulnerable, so I said, "Can I think about it?"

Her face went pale like she'd seen a Gaboon viper, and she squeezed my paw. "I know it's a big commitment. Take all the time you need." She held out some runny egg on her finger for me to lick off, and I thought she'd understood my fear. But then she spent the rest of the morning alone on the deck, staring at the surf crashing against the rocks.

After that, the subject never came up again. She'd seen me all right. This time maybe she didn't like what she saw. Looking back, do I wish I'd just gone with it, taken the risk? You bet. But there's no rewind in life. You can't put the colobus back in the tree once you've ripped off its head, as my mother liked to say.

The scripts got worse. Jane and I fought the screenwriters, but those were really proxy fights with His Lordship about who deserved credit for what back in Africa. His name was on the picture, so I don't have to tell you who won. At least he was a professional on the set. I'll give him that.

One Saturday morning, we'd planned a drive up Highway 1 with Marlene Dietrich to get some fresh air, but by the time she came over, I'd already had a few too many to get behind the wheel. "Why don't you sleep it off?" Jane said. "The two of us will be back by sundown, and we'll all go out to dinner." That was fine by me. I wasn't crazy about Germans. I'd met some nasty ones in Africa. Did you know when Kipling wrote, "Lesser races without the law," he was talking about German colonists, not the locals? Around eight o'clock, I woke up to the phone ringing, and it was

Jane saying the car had broken down and the two of them were spending the night at a motel in Isla Vista. I didn't see her again until a week later, when she came by for her clothes.

I didn't handle it gracefully. She was wearing a new pair of silver bracelets. "I like your handcuffs," I said. "Does she chain you to the wall at night, like those diamond thieves back in Opar? If a certain chimpanzee hadn't shimmied down a vine with the key, your flat Baltimore ass would still be hanging there."

"Don't spoil the memories," she said. "You're going to need them some day." She ran her hand over my occipital bump one last time and left me. I turned my back on all of apedom for her, and she left me. Give me a minute, would you? This hot wind gets in my eyes, makes a mess of them.

Anyway, that's how we killed the goose that laid the golden egg. Word got around Hollywood that none of the three of us would work with each other, so the studio called it quits on our jungle adventures. I'd been looking forward to doing serious drama for a change, but suddenly, it was like I had dengue fever, and no one would touch me. People came by my table at Ciro's and said, "They typecast you, the lousy so-and-sos. That should have been you in *Treasure of the Sierra Madre*." But in truth, I was in no shape to make a picture. Losing Jane wrecked me. The only silver lining was that I was finally free of His Lordship, or so I thought.

But of course, true to form, the bastard returned.

He drove up to my house in his Bentley, come to rub it in, I thought. "Terribly sorry to hear it, old boy. Women. Damned fickle things, you know." He'd taken elocution lessons by then so that he could talk like an English lord off screen. He also favored a gray three-piece suit in wool and a fedora.

"Who asked you?" I said. I stood in my doorway, a bottle of rye in one paw and an eight-by-ten glossy of my lost love in the other, taking in the affront of his civilization. "You're wearing spats. For thirty years you don't even wear shoes, now you're wearing spats. Spats are bullshit. That car is bullshit." I tried to slam the door on him, but I fell over instead. "You're bullshit," I said into the carpet.

He carried me to the shower and turned on the cold water for ten minutes. Then he poured a pot of black coffee down my throat, wrapped me up in a blanket, put me in the back of his fine piece of British engineering, drove me to the clinic himself, and gave them his signed check with the amount left blank.

I don't think he felt one drop of guilt. It was just his character. He had a savior complex, so he rescued you. It's what he did. He was a preening racist, sexist, humanist jackass, and not much of an actor, but he rescued you. And this story, which was supposed to be about me and Jane, somehow ends with a close-up of him. I hate that son of a bitch.

Kala

Oh, what an ugly baby! You hear that a lot. It's a joke. In a way, all babies are ugly, with scrunched-up faces and weird, oversized heads, but at the same time babies are the most beautiful thing in the world, and no one really can have an ugly baby. Except me. I really did.

I'd lost my first baby, you see. He fell. It wasn't my fault. Or maybe it was, but it happened constantly, so I was permitted to think it wasn't my fault. Sometimes I think we were all out of our damn minds. Everyone knew the statistics, how many falling deaths a year, the injuries, the costs, the burden on the whole system. We could have done something about it, but there was no real will. Every time it seemed like we were making progress, some old silverback would say, "What are you going to do, not live in a tree?" And everyone laughed and regurgitated some fruit and nothing got done. It made me so mad I couldn't see straight. Now, what I wouldn't do to have those kinds of problems again.

But then I found a new baby. Hairless. Pale skin. Eyes the color of the ocean when it's raining. Weird, shrunken teeth, when they finally came in. The ugliest baby ever seen. I remember the day at the wooden cabin by the shore when I snatched him away from Kerchak's terrible fists and fed him at my breast. I said to myself, what are you doing, going from one baby to the next? You must be off your coconut. This is the grief speaking. Take some *you* time before you plunge back into motherhood. But I felt my milk flow into him, felt his need. That's a heady feeling, to give something life, even something so ugly. From that day on, he took life from me, from all of us. I never thought he'd take so much.

He was a slow child. So slow, he didn't seem to grow at all for a long time. Those were the hardest years. Everyone said, "Kala, you're a gorgeous young ape. You've got decades of fertility ahead of you, and you're wasting yourself on this lump. There are some nice low branches near the hyena dell. Put him on one of those. The hyenas are professionals. They'll know how to take care of him. This doesn't have to be on you."

I had to advocate for him so hard! "No," I said, "he's learning in his own time. He has his own intelligence. You don't know his potential. I see progress every day." I was lying to them and to myself. Inside, I felt hopeless.

My husband, Tublat, was the worst. He'd look at my little white-skinned baby clinging to the branch of a kola nut tree and shake his head in disgust. I know he was thinking about infanticide—which is perfectly healthy and normal for guys, but still, hard not to take personally. To be fair, my husband suffered. His friends tossed leaves behind his back because he was raising another male's child. He couldn't even pretend it was his. When life was all bamboo shoots and larvae, he'd say, "At least he's a hominid," and give me a sad, weak appeasement grin. But if it was rainy season, or a drought, or Sabor the lioness had just eaten his running buddy, he'd beat his chest, tear up vegetation, and scream, "When do we get to have a child of our own? A healthy, normal baby with fangs. Is that too much to ask?" I'd be breaking open a termite mound and he'd come up from behind, grab my paws, and hold me tight. "I want to mount you right now, in front of the whole troop," he'd grunt in my ear. "I want them all to hear my copulatory pants. Ooh, ooh, ooh!" He was a hopeless romantic, and of course I'd be tempted. But I'd think of my little White-Skin, think of how special our bond was, and know I didn't want another baby to come between us.

Years passed before he was strong enough to even hold a vine, let alone swing from one to another. But that first time he launched himself off a branch, reached out and made the transfer, sweet Jesus, the pride I felt. There's nothing like a baby's first swing. I wanted to climb the highest tree and bark it to the whole world. And then, suddenly, he grew like a cassava vine, and he was flying around in the trees all day. I fell in love with him all over again, and I was so happy, for a time.

If only it hadn't been for that damn cabin. I can't remember exactly when he started sneaking off, spending hours by himself in there with the door locked. I thought, he's in that awkward stage, he needs privacy, it's just a phase. He'd get that sly expression on his face, and Tublat would look up from his sweet potato and say, "Boy, just where the hell do you think you're going?"

"Leave him alone!" I'd say. "He's got good judgment. I trust him." Then I'd turn to my beloved adopted son. "Go ahead. Tell your father what you're doing."

"I'm just looking at stuff. You know, checking out the strange black bugs on the folded white leaves, things like that. Geez Louise, you'd think I pooped in the waterhole or something."

Looking back now, I wish I'd broken his fingers.

I don't have to tell you what was really going on in that cabin. He was using tools. You make a mark with a pencil, the next thing you know you're using a knife, and then suddenly you're behind the wheel of a tractor and the jungle is going, going, gone. Those black bugs on white leaves? He was teaching himself to read. A knife kills an animal. A book kills a continent.

He went out to that cabin a healthy, sweet, innocent primate and came back a sociopath. That's when he started his hanging fetish. He'd work a vine into a loop, sneak out on a tree limb, wait for one of us to come along, drop the loop around his neck, and half choke the life out of him. For fun. I wanted to die. I try not to think about it, but it comes back on me when I least expect. I'll see him with that sick, human smile on his face, legs gripping the branch, pulling back hard, strangling one of his own family. I guess by then we weren't family anymore. He'd learned better. He saw *us* in those books. A is for Ape. Something lesser. B is for Boy. Something greater.

He came sauntering around upright one day with his hair cut short, his face shaved, and—God, I still blush to say it—his genitals covered. "You little son-of-a-woman," Tublat said. "You're an embarrassment to the Mangani race. I can't stand to see you like that. Where's your sense of decency? Answer me, boy!"

"Don't hit him!" I cried. But it was too late. Tublat cuffed him hard across his brow ridge.

My son just took it and looked back slowly. "I'll remember that," he said, and he walked off into the bush. You could say he never came back. Not my son, anyway.

You know what happened next. He took over the troop using human devices—nooses, knives, full nelsons. He killed Kerchak and became the new alpha. Then when Terzak challenged him, my son didn't kill him; he did something even worse. He brought humiliation to the jungle. He made Terzak say Kagoda—I submit.

That night at the Dum Dum, my son said, "I am the King of the Apes, mighty hunter, mighty fighter. In all the jungle there is none so great." And all my alleged friends sat there with big fruit-eating grins on their face and said, "Huh! You are great." I should have tanned his arrogant little white heinie. But it was too late for that. He crouched there in the moonlight on that big rock, drinking it in, like blood straight from the jugular.

And then more humans came in a ship, and my son went off with them into the world and did many things, versions of which you may have heard, or read, or watched. I didn't think much of them. Neither did the guy who wrote them. He said, "If people were paid for writing rot such as I read in some of those magazines, I could write stories just as rotten." Yet I felt pride. My son was famous, and people all over the world loved him. I took that as a consolation from afar. It hurts too much for me to speak it now, but his name became legend. You know it.

What you don't know is that decades later he returned.

He came with men and machines and a troop of his own called Grey-stoke Agricultural. He came for those damn kola nuts. All those years we'd chewed them and gotten a harmless little buzz. Now they were worth money. Morality in the jungle was based on primal needs. Whatever you did to eat, drink, mate, and survive was right. Human morality was different. It included the need for fizzy, sweet beverages.

There was pushback, of course. Mbonga's grandson was working with an NGO by then, and he got the area declared a World Heritage site because we were endangered. Commercial exploitation to be severely restricted. In an office building in London, my son and his new friends pondered that development and came up with an elegant solution. No apes, no restrictions. The lucky ones got shot. Those of us who weren't so lucky got trapped. Excuse me—rescued. I was rescued.

Now I'm a featured resident of the Greystoke Foundation for the Preservation of Wildlife just outside London. I hope you appreciate the irony. I know I do. They don't use kola nuts for soda anymore, but they discovered palm oil and petroleum, and the whole place—well, you wouldn't recognize it now. There's no home to go back to, even if I could.

So here I sit behind bars, in this foggy, cold island far from the continent I love, looking out at the twisted parade of men and women in lab coats and the occasional university group. At least I have a job. They paint a dot on my forehead, put me in front of a mirror, and wait to see if I touch the dot. Sometimes I do, sometimes I don't. I like to mess with their heads. They got me addicted to sugar, so now I have to unscrew lids or put boxes on top of boxes to get at their precious M&Ms. Droll, right?

They taught me a new language. That's a positive, I suppose. When you acquire a new language, you acquire a new self. But what's the good of language when no one listens?

He came by the other day for a few minutes, my son. It was a very big deal. They cleared the place out, and he came stumping in, half a dozen of his troop behind him. Bodyguards. A photographer. A videographer. Some young woman who recorded everything he said with her phone. I could tell from his disregard that he mounts her. He's much older now, but I suppose I am too. I never thought I'd live so long. He got fat and walks with a cane. Yes, it's made of ivory. His hair is white, and he wears a moustache. It looks like someone glued an albino caterpillar to his face. Still, he seems worth ten of any other human to me. His shoulders are broad and heavy. His nose twitches—I see him unconsciously register my scent. You can take the boy out of the jungle . . .

Yet when he pulls up in front of my white-walled prison and shades his eyes against the bright lab lights with his hand, he peers in at me like he's never in his life seen an animal other than a corgi.

I speak plainly to him in the language of his youth. Save me, I say. Free me. I am your mother. I fed you at my breast. I taught you how to peel the bark from the bamboo and suck the goodness within. I taught you the ritual of the Dum Dum. When Bolgani the gorilla nearly killed you, I nursed you back to life. I licked your wounds, brushed flies from them, brought you water in my mouth. No human mother could have shown more unselfish and sacrificing devotion.

He says nothing, so I resort to the language they have taught me.

"Mother," I sign, and point to myself. "Baby," I sign, and point to him. "Remember."

"My Lord," my keeper says. "It's just as I said. Our research shows that they have a rudimentary sense of the passage of time. She's telling you she remembers she was once fertile and had offspring."

"Splendid," my son says. "Extraordinary work you're doing here. Immensely valuable. The more we understand of these creatures, the more we shall understand of ourselves."

"Yes," my keeper says. "That's exactly the point, isn't it."

My son moves on, his hands waving away his chattering flunkies with human clumsiness, fluent now in the language of forgetting.

EDWARD PORTER's short fiction has appeared in *Glimmer Train,* *The Hudson Review, The Gettysburg Review, Colorado Review, Booth, Barrelhouse, Catamaran, Best New American Voices,* and elsewhere. He holds an MFA from Warren Wilson College and a PhD from the University of Houston. He has been a Madison, MacDowell, and Stegner Fellow and has taught creative writing at Millsaps College. Currently he is a Jones Lecturer in Fiction at Stanford University.

2

JOHN THORNTON SPEAKS

Pam Houston

After Call of the Wild.

I never figured love would be part of the equation for me. I was too shy to talk to women, and men didn't interest me like that. An only child born to older parents, I joined the Third Cavalry to get away from my father's fists and wound up down on the Mexican border fighting the Garzistas. We rode into San Ygnacio nine days after the massacre there, just enough time for the smell of the bodies and burned buildings to have reached a crescendo under the desert winter sun. In '93, when the revolution was put down and the leaders arrested, I went to the Yukon to freeze out the ghosts I'd collected in Texas.

The big country to the North of Everything has terms of its own that are more clear and comprehensible than anything in either my father's house or the South Texas desert. It's cold here, often brutally so, and if you lose your concentration the cold will kill you. There's more open land than your imagination can run to and more animals a man can eat than them that want to eat a man, though there are plenty of those as well. After my first winter up here, I decided I could live with the terms of the Yukon.

It's hard to wake up to the way the air smells up here and not find yourself hopping out of bed with a whistle on your lips, hard to hear the crack and ping of the breakup on the river without your mouth curling into a grin. There's gold in the streams for those willing to persist, though for me, the pursuit of gold has always been more excuse than reason, like the way a man will put a fishing pole in his hand for an excuse to walk a stream. A man is a puny thing in the face of all this frozen rock and ice, and even the mountains that rise to nineteen thousand feet are puny compared to the weather. The wind howls a hundred miles an hour through this valley sometimes, and it can bring near a hundred inches of snow in a single night. When the storm moves out, the skies clear and the temperatures fall to sixty below zero, and the only thing to keep you warm on those nights is the sight of the Northern Lights, dancing in green and yellow and crimson veils across the sky. We lose most all our daylight in December, but come March it's returning so fast every day seems like cause for celebration. Spring rolls into summer, the days lengthening and lengthening until it seems like you've been sitting around the campfire with a beer in your hand watching the twilight all your life. Then one day the wild blueberries are ripe, and the tundra goes all gold and vermillion, and the dogs prick up their ears as they wait for the first flurries that usher in the season in which they get to do the thing they were born for.

What I'm trying to say is that once I got here, I never could get myself to leave because I was always afraid to miss the season that was coming. What I'm trying to say is that the Yukon taught me how to look forward. It stirred something in my chest that other people might call hope.

Growing up in my father's house taught me to be vigilant, and vigilance is high on the list of skills needed to survive up here. But everybody makes mistakes, and I made one, too: took a team too far from camp one February day when warm water pooled on the surface of the river. We were a good thirty miles from camp when the wind picked up and a good ten miles out when we smacked into a full-on blizzard. I didn't notice my mukluks were soaked through till they froze solid as iron. The only thing I'll say for myself is that I did take time that night to make sure the dogs were in better shape than I was. The only one who returned to camp the next morning with frostbite because of my stupidity was me.

I'd been hobbling around talking to myself for a good two months when the abomination another man called a dog sled rounded the river bend below my camp, with Buck leading a team of half-dead and starving dogs up the Yukon, which had been creaking and cracking and screaming against itself all day.

I've had to hold my own in a barroom brawl or two since I've been up here, and I engaged in a little hand-to-hand combat in Texas, but when I hung up my Cavalry coat, I took a vow for all time to be done with killing. Committing an act of violence against another man, I have come to understand, is not evidence of strength but of fear, of inadequacy. Committing an act of violence against a dog, one who has pulled you, all your ill-chosen items, and your fat-assed sister halfway from Skagway to Dawson when you've not brought the means to feed it enough by half— well, there are words for what that is a sign of, but I will not utter them.

When such a man rounded the river bend, the whip heavy on his starving, limping team, my first inclination was to stay out of it and let the fools drown in the Yukon. I'll never know if the fact that Buck chose that moment to decide he would rather lie down and be beaten to death with a club than take another step on that man's behalf was divine providence or accident. I am not beyond believing that even from the distance of thirty yards, Buck was the sort of dog who could sense I needed him in my life as much as he needed me in his. What I do know for certain is if that moronic brute who held the club had challenged me when I cut Buck out of his traces and led him into my camp, in spite of all my vows of pacifism, I would have slit his throat.

In the weeks that followed, Buck and I healed together, and it wasn't long before he revealed his extraordinary nature. Buck is a giant, nearly four feet at the shoulder and 175 pounds, now that he's eating right, but he is even larger in heart than in body. Intelligent, of course, but also wise, an old wisdom come down through centuries. Loyal, proud, and contemplative. Soon after his arrival, I learned to follow his gaze, endeavored to see what he saw, be it danger around a bend—say a bull moose in a rage, disguising itself in some alders—or some small example of the world's bright beauty. The way the sun played along the mercuried surface of the silt-swollen river in the afternoon, for example, seemed especially pleasing to him. In this way, Buck taught me to favor my intuition over my intellect, and, at least momentarily, to release all judgment, of *self* and otherwise, and just *be*. Every time he took my hand in his mouth and bit down, just hard enough to hurt a little—never harder—I knew he was letting me know he was my brother, and no man on earth could wish for a more soulful brother than he.

You have all read the story of how he saved me from the river in flood stage, how he broke out a sled carrying a thousand pounds of flour to win a bet I was foolish enough to have made. But if you have been lucky enough in your life to be loved wholly and truly by a dog, you know that feats of strength and endurance pale in comparison to the moment that beast's kind eye falls upon you and you are seen in a way that you have never been seen before. Whatever mistakes you have made, whatever ill you have done, and more impressively, whatever ill you have let be done to you, is not so much forgiven as made irrelevant in a love that pure. And when he comes and rests his heavy head on your thigh and sighs long and deep, when he leans in for a scratch behind the ears that makes him groan with pleasure, he is telling you that you are not, have never been, and never will be alone in this world, for you and he are a pack of two.

PAM HOUSTON is the author of two collections of linked short stories, *Cowboys Are My Weakness* and *Waltzing the Cat*. Her stories have been selected for the 1999 volumes of *Best American Short Stories*, *The O. Henry Awards*, and *The Pushcart Prize*, and she is a regular contributor to *O, the Oprah Magazine*, the *New York Times*, *Bark*, *More*, and many other periodicals. A collection of autobiographical essays, *A Little More About Me*, was published in 1999, and a novel, *Sight Hound*, in 2005. Houston has edited a collection of fiction, nonfiction, and poetry for Ecco Press called *Women on Hunting*, and she has written the text for a book of photographs called *Men Before Ten A.M.* Her novel *Contents May Have Shifted* was released in 2012.

3

ISLAND OF THE KINGSBRIDE

Molly Gutman

YOU COULD BE THE BRIDE OF THE KING, JUST AS ANYONE COULD be the bride of the king. All you would need is a father, which most people have, and that father would need to hate you. Maybe as a child you broke a bottle of Johnny Walker while playing near the pantry. Maybe you were so beautiful that your mother died of jealousy, a trope no less real because of its inclusion in fairy tales. Maybe this, his sale of you, was his final act of vengeance.

But enough of him. This is about you.

To hear the picture tell it, you were an actress, a poor one, and that's why you boarded the boat. Of course, it's all nonsense.

EXT. DOCK—NIGHT
Two men, FATHER and THE DIRECTOR, meet on a dock at night under the buzz of a marina lamppost. Both wear slick leather hats. Fog rolls thickly in and smells like salt fish; the men shift and, unilluminated, they become invisible. One man leaves, his coat pockets heavy with money, and the other leaves with YOU.

The voyage is of no particular note; you were treated well enough and fed. You can lie if you want, say you were never touched. Here, think instead of the first time you spotted the island: the barely discernible crush of scrub that, like a rip, appeared between the horizon and atmosphere. The toothy line of trees was a color-sucking black. The wind over the water sounded like it was screaming for you to jump, but you ignored it. You credited the unease in your stomach to the pitching of the boat.

Perhaps in those early days you were a little naïve; surely you can admit this. But still you saw through your captor's pitch on the picture in two shakes flat. He said he wanted to make a nature film, but no one comes all the way out here to film a pretty lady framed by exotic trees. A bald lie, one you were slick enough to catch. And yet, later, when you're still on the island and he isn't anymore, yes, he'll make a film about you. The film will do you no justice whatsoever, but then again, very little will.

THE DIRECTOR Come on, sugar. Let's hear a scream.

YOU Perhaps you should ask Mary Philbin; I am to understand her screams are quite recordable. Great for films. She can even change pitch on command.

THE DIRECTOR A lesser man might say I'd give you something what to scream for.

YOU Or who played Elizabeth Frankenstein? A shame you don't have her instead.

THE DIRECTOR This may just make you famous. You and me both, darlin'. You want that?

YOU Mae Clark. I just now remembered.

You were right to see through his sales pitch. He is a director, sure, but this is no location for filming. Or at least no location for him to film; you see it in his sneer as he walks you down the ramp, in his wrinkled nose at the locals, in all the glances over his shoulder. His ragged nails pinch the flesh of your arm. Your flesh whines in response; his nails are drawing blood. You choose not to look.

Off the boat you see men but no women. Some of the men have sad, hollow faces, like you remind them of something. Years ahead, when you finally leave, you will learn why they watched you like that, and if you're honest you already know: the reason you see no women on the island is that the island has none left to offer. The island has depleted even its girls. A thin, short man bursts into tears at the sight of you.

The king has never been without bride; they are terrified of how he might act. They have offered the director a large sum of money to bring a replacement. Much larger than what he paid for you; he's making a considerable profit.

EXT. JUNGLE—LATE EVENING
Dark. Hazy. Cacophony of bugs. YOU are chained between two trees. YOU are wispy, blonde, wearing the only dress you came with, alone in the woods. A large rustle moves closer, and the leaves tremble.

The king has a face like a wire brush. He is a giant gorilla with quite the human posture, gray and silver, and of at least sixty feet. His eyes are keen. He bows low to you, very low, and there on the top of his head, you see the tiniest of hats pinned to the slicked-flat part of his gorilla hair. He has made an effort to look nice, to impress you, even though you've just been sold to him and have no say in the matter. He has brought a flower, a giant wild spiky thing, and he passes it to you. In your chains, you cannot hold it, and anyway the thing is as big as your head and stinks. The stem is taller than you are.

He tries tucking it under your arm, and when that doesn't work, he lays it down easy on the dirt. You will grow to hate these flowers. He unwraps your chains.

All you see, when he attempts a smile, are those excruciating teeth, plastered with leaves. Hard not to imagine your bones wedged in there, isn't it? Your own bones and the shreds of your dress; his gaze exposes you, turns you translucent. You think of funerals. You think of how your father must have hated you. You do not scream. You do not scream.

The tall woods part like they're bowing to you, or to him, probably him. Your legs drape over the log of his arm and your back props against his chest as he takes giant gorilla steps between nut trees and humongous shrubs. His chest is damp and wiry. Sweat plasters your hair to your face. You have taken few trains in your life, but now you're moving fast as one; the trees sweep past you at alarming speed. But the only direction you're looking is down. From your swinging, sticky roost, all you think is how far it would be to drop.

YOU   Where are we going?

THE KING   (pants)

YOU   Slow down. You owe me speech, at least.

THE KING   Rrrrrrr. Rrr.

YOU   Good God. Are we heading to the river? Slow down!

THE KING   Rooooo. Rrrrriv. Rrr.

He carries you, wedding style, over the threshold of the river; he wades to the knees in the wild, loud water. Over there is a bridge he does not use. The water foams and parts around his legs, like it might around boulders. And he exits just as steadily as he entered, and he wipes each foot neatly on the grass to dry them off, and he continues to carry you away. Your father's voice in your head says this is your imminent death, but deep in your bones comes a stranger, more terrifying thought: this is your imminent home.

EXT. JUNGLE—AFTERNOON

The shafts of light that have reached the forest floor are trick swords in a magician's act, punching through the canopy at all angles. The air is so humid that at all hours water beads on the broadleaves; when the beads tip off and fall, they turn to emeralds. YOU can pick these up and collect them, if YOU wish; they are hard, clear emeralds, of value perhaps to some, but for YOU just beautiful artifacts. So much is beautiful and dangerous here. Someone small living here, like YOU, needs always to be cautious of falling emeralds.

You are days into marriage, maybe weeks. It's hard to tell. You only think the word *marriage* when it sneaks up on you. Otherwise you think of it as *the arrangement*, and that's how you phrase it when you speak to him. I want no part of the arrangement, you've said a hundred times, and then he grows sulky and violent and you change your wording: What, exactly, does he plan to get out of the arrangement? But you know the answer—you are glad he never responds. You are aching from the inside out; that is the answer. Right now he is gone somewhere, and you are high in a tree, an ankle chained to the branch, using an emerald you hid in your brassiere to sharpen your nails. The idea of claws delights you. They feel like ballast, in a way: your sharp, hard nails against the tender bruises that line your legs. Drag those claws along your own palm to feel the knife of you; rake them against the branch of your seat to hear the scrape of you.

The woods stir, and you look up high to watch for his face emerging from the leaves. If you had been an actress, like the picture will one day claim you are, you at least would have wanted a handsomer counterpart. Preferably one who did not believe that he owned you. Preferably one who did not cover your small body with his and thereby do unspeakable damage. But his face never appears; his gargantuan body never steps into the clearing.

Instead the minuscule figure of the director emerges far below. From your position in the tree, he looks like a broken twig.

Seems he has left the island and come back; his sale of you, which, yes, made him rich, has not been enough. He wants you to return with him, to be filmed in some souped-up picture based loosely on your life here. You know the type, a film where your neckline is too low and the king is too handsome, or too gruesome. It will be quite the attraction, he assures you, and he would be happy to usher some of the money in your direction.

He asks you where your husband is, and your insides mineralize at the word, and you tell him you don't know. You and the director are far away from each other and have to raise your voices in order to be understood. English falls out of use more easily than you might have expected. You haven't been given much say lately, and you take the little bit you can:

YOU How do you rrr, prr, propose convincing him?

THE DIRECTOR I don't think you understand, honey. This could make you rich. I know I said that last time, but now I really mean it. Honest. A star, and him, too. Men have a way of figuring this out; I'll make him understand.

YOU I say no. He'll say no. I say no.

THE DIRECTOR It's happening one way or another. If you don't come, we'll make a story of you yet. I'll say he carried you to the top of a tower and dropped you off. It'll be a hit. I'll find him now to strike a deal. See you soon, sweetheart.

He will not see you soon, no, but he is right that the picture will make it big. A woman prettier than you will play your part, and a machine will play the king's. Try not to think about it; instead imagine that, as the director recedes back into the shadow of brush, he bumps against one of the giant ankles of his target. Imagine that your captor pinches the director between his large thumb and finger and relocates the man to his mouth; imagine the crunch of bones against massive molars. In reality, the exchange is less dramatic, though still the director leaves without what he wants. He would like to own everything, sell everything, and while the world works largely in this vein—you, now, are proof of this— you also know this model is unsustainable. Please, take heart. This model is unsustainable.

EXT. JUNGLE—SUNSET
Sunset stabs through broad-leaved hardwoods. A ray of orange illuminates the plates YOU have laid on a rough table; the berry-stewed brown birds are edged in gold and look delectable. Jungle quiet. Humidity shimmers. YOU have gems of sweat on your face. A bouquet of three spiky flowers jut from a hole THE KING has dug in the ground, the only vase large enough to hold them. Still their huge petals reach taller than the table. THE KING takes up a whole side of the table, YOU small as a speck on the other. Body language suggests this, the stewed birds and the picked flowers, are usual sights.

He is more human than the director later makes him out to be. The film, when they produce it in a few years, shows him as all gorilla and strength, which yes, is true, but also you see a wit to him and a knack for first impressions. Yet, on the same hand, he believes he can own you and has done you repeated violence. Surely your bruises are proof enough of this, if your chains aren't. History is complicated in this way.

You have taken a while to prepare. You have been gathering bright, tiny toads for days. In the spirit of things, you have honed your claws to points and oiled them with bird fat, so they glint in the deepening light.

He takes his plate and tips the bird down his throat, like he always does. You pick off a wing of yours and bite as delicately as you know how. You are chewing as he registers the extra weight he swallowed; you take a sip of water as he begins to cough. It is a deep, rooting kind of sound.

The toads have infected the lining of his esophagus; all blood to his brain is cutting off. Thunder as he tumbles from his seat. He blinks at you, his eyes soggy, and into them you smile a kind of accidental smile. Only then, in his last slip of consciousness, does he piece together that the toads were of your doing, that you slipped each one lovingly into the cavity of his bird, using a waxy leaf for a glove.

A titanic hand rises to his chest. He emits fat tears.

His eyes dull and his lips blue, and the tears slipping to the grass harden into diamonds. You take those diamonds. You fix them in your knotted hair.

To hear the picture tell it, only helicopters and machine guns and militaries could subdue him. Only you know the truth: that it was so much easier. That you are more capable than helicopters and militaries. You are more capable than machine guns.

You place one kiss on his bottom lip, the very first one you've initiated.

And then you slice that lip with your index nail and slip into the dark of the woods.Leaves blur past you at exhilarating speed. Branches and limbs bow out of your way as you jump top to top; now you are the queen of the trees, and they act accordingly.

EXT. JUNGLE—NIGHT
Your silhouette floats across the bridge. From afar, the diamonds in your hair catch moonlight. And up the trees YOU go.

The wind is not rushing past your ears; you are the wind. You test a scream and find that it feels better than any battle cry:

YOU Rrr. Raaa. Awrgh-ah! Aheeee!

MOLLY GUTMAN earned her MFA from the University of Nevada, Reno. You can find her stories and poems in *Black Warrior Review, Fairy Tale Review, Salt Hill, Mid-American Review,* and elsewhere.

4

WHAT THE FIRE GOD SAID TO THE BEASTS

Michael Poore

(Being a story of Captain Ahab, before ever he was a captain, as related by his particular friend, the hunchback John Pitch.)

"It's only an island if you look at it from the water," I said that first morning.

We sat on a high rock, watching the sea.

Ahab laughed the way he did, like a mad dog barking, and clapped his hands together.

"Thou makest the best of things, Pitch," he said. "Taken on its own merits, an island may as well be a whole world. Thou hast a glad soul, which is a fine thing."

A fine thing indeed, considering our condition. Considering the hurricane, considering our ship was a pile of toothpicks on the ocean bottom, considering we, ourselves, were toothpicks and rags, torn and bloodied from swimming in over the razor coral.

"Glad or not," I said, "my soul is hungry and needs watering."

He barked again and rose to his feet, and we staggered together into the jungle to see what we could manage by way of staying alive.

We discussed things as we went, trying to be reasonable and educated. Fresh water, we knew, would come from the direction of the high ground. Ahab had learned from the Shawnee how to trap fish. As for shelter, we didn't know yet if we would find caves or make something clever out of sticks.

"And there's the other matter," Ahab growled.

The "other matter" made my bowels uneasy.

It was something the cook had said aboard the lifeboat. We had no sooner sighted land, after two weeks adrift in the one surviving whaleboat, than he told how he knew these islands from sailors' tales, and how men who were shipwrecked would turn and swim back out to sea rather than dare those shores.

And Ahab had said, "Pray why, cook?" and was told, "Those that live there. They eat men."

It was an honest dilemma, much debated about the whaleboat, whether to chance being eaten or give the island a miss in hopes of intercepting another whaler. When votes were cast to remain on the ocean, Ahab, who had been manning the steering oar, stood and said, "Well, one of ye will need to mind the sweep. I'm for taking my chances ashore," and he dove over the gunwale into the waves.

Ahab had been my boon companion since I was fourteen. His good sense and reason, in those days, were as solid as an old stone church, and I trusted him. Over the side with me! The others rowed away, and God knows what became of them. As for me, once I was in the water, my only thought was for my friend and myself and how we might contrive to stay out of the grave a while longer.

In the jungle, now, this remained my focus.

We would find a way to eat and stay dry. We would avoid the island's landlords, if we could, until delivered by Providence or some genius of our own.

With cannibals in mind, we did our best to go quietly as we searched for signs of water. Even if we hadn't been cautious, I don't know that we could have been heard over the million voices of the jungle itself. Such a racket! Buzzings and woop-woops and flutterings of all sorts! The sounds of horrid, pale things in holes. Sure enough, as we paused to rest, something ambushed and killed something else. There was a sudden thrash of leaves and a wild scream followed by a grim and particular silence.

"God's teeth," said I to Ahab. "Here's an end to us, I think."

"If that's so," he answered, "just as well to be eaten by something and prove useful."

I shuddered at that, and we forged on. Shoving vines aside. Clambering over deadfalls and jagged volcanic stones. My hunched shoulder bothered me, somewhat, but I set my jaw and said nothing. I'd gone twenty years with crooked bones and been a hunter and a whaleman. One pain or two, I determined, wouldn't kill me in the jungle. A lack of fresh water was more likely to do that.

If you've ever been near to dying of thirst, you know that a person gets to feeling like he's made of sand inside. Movement of any kind becomes hard work, every joint like a rusted hinge. So when dark clouds swooped in and dimmed the sun, we whispered prayers and were hopeful.

Indeed, minutes later, lightning strobed the jungle.

Thunder followed at a distance.

At the same time, my eye caught on something of interest, through a break in the trees, to port. A steep hillside with a scattering of tall boulders at the top. Ahab saw it, too, and we tacked in that direction until we found ourselves somewhat sheltered by overhanging rocks, hidden from view on three sides.

Here, we finally caught our breath.

I stole a look at my friend, the most constant companion of my life, perhaps about to accompany me in death as well, and do you know what he was doing, that mystery of New England? Reaching into his trousers and fishing out his damned clay pipe, is what. Only Ahab, beset with storms and sinkings and—perhaps—men who wanted to eat him, would somehow manage not to lose his clay pipe. (I wanted to ask if he had a loaf of rye bread and a lonely widow in his pocket, too.) Closing his teeth around the stem, he surveyed the jungle and the approaching weather like a man at home in his slippers.

"They'll eat thee first, I should think," he said. "They'll be curious. Might even think thee a new species," and so saying, he gave me an affectionate clap upon my hump.

Now that we had come to a stop again, a profound fatigue settled on us. I proposed we dig in for a while and gather what strength we had.

"Wise old Pitch," said Ahab.

I volunteered to stand the first watch. He agreed, folded himself up on the sand, and seemed at peace. Maybe he even snored. I wouldn't know, because I was asleep myself in a trice, standing up straight as a post.

It was the rain that woke me.

Not just humble old wet rain but rain like a whip, hurled by a ferocious wind.

Lightning! A flash like a cannonade! *Thunder!* Also like a cannonade.

I had thrown my head back and opened my mouth to receive a deluge of fat, delicious rain when my brain caught up with my senses and I realized that sleeping Ahab and I no longer had our rocky home to ourselves. For among the rocks—*flash!*—I now clearly saw, were people.

People. Men. Islanders. Men dressed in the way islanders are accustomed to dress, which is to say not much or not at all, and ornamented with paints and leaves and feathers and tattoos.

"Sheep and gravestones," I muttered.

I moved to give sleeping Ahab a kick, but fresh lightning showed him awake and standing, addressing the tallest, most heavily decorated of our hosts.

"*Talofa!*" he shouted over the rain and thunder. "*O au o se i'afiafia!*"

He was employing a kind of pidgin dialect, a chimera bred by sailors from pieces heard anywhere from Polynesia to China. You could sometimes make yourself understood among strange peoples if you used a lot of gestures, although it was difficult, if not impossible, to be fluent.

"You're a happy fish," I said to Ahab. "I think that's what you said."

"Could be. I hope not."

The tall islander frowned. We all frowned.

"*O le a soumanatu e, iluga o lonatauau?*" one of them asked.

This translated loosely into "What's wrong with his shoulder?"

They all started doing hunchback imitations and laughing.

"Starboard," said Ahab out the side of his mouth.

I gave him a look.

"Run," he said, "to starboard, quick as thee can."

We sprang across the sand. In an instant, the islanders lunged after, raising spears—

But something happened.

Something powerful. Something like the sun bursting down on us.

Something, followed by an equally powerful nothing.

↯

I woke up in a shadowy hut with a woman leaning over me. Her eyes were the first thing I saw, and they scared me. Bright and wide they were, and seemed to shine from the inside out like a star does.

"*Talofa*," said I.

"*Talofa* yourself," she answered. "You've been asleep for three days. Enough's enough; I'm afraid you're going to piss all over my floor."

I realized that my body was sending me a variety of urgent signals. My stomach felt seasick. I was thirsty. I was sore. I smelled like old porridge.

With all this discomfort, I didn't know whether I was capable of standing, much less walking. But I managed to gain my feet and stagger outside, where I emptied myself in every way that is natural to man into a patch of weeds.

I observed that I was naked.

Damn. When a pair of torn trousers is all a man has in the world, he minds when they go missing.

After cleaning myself with a handful of *pukii* leaves, I turned to get an idea of my surroundings. To get an idea of *anything*. What had happened? What was going to happen next? Where were my pants?

My surroundings were a few huts raised a little on bamboo stilts. Jungle beyond.

The woman with the big bright eyes watched me from her door.

The eyes, it turned out, were not her only notable feature. She was, as far as I could tell, a woman of middle years. For clothing, she was wrapped around the waist in something like a leather sheath, and besides this she was naked. An unusual species of nakedness, though. Not vulnerable but proud. She was naked the way a sixty-gun frigate is naked.

It occurred to me, at this point, to wonder what had become of Ahab.

I cleared my throat and said, "My friend?"

My reply was a voice behind me, saying, "Here's Ahab, Pitch, in his purest form."

Joy! I turned to find my boonsman emerging from the trees, naked as a stick of firewood, carrying a bundle of long, green grass over his shoulder.

"You live!" I gladly observed.

"Follow!" he said, clapping me on the hump. "I've got breakfast."

And on he walked, tossing a nod to the woman before entering one of the huts. I followed.

Inside, he let his bundle fall to the earthen floor, and a couple of breadfruit rolled free.

We sat and ate. My stomach, quickly calming, was ravenous.

"Lightning," said Ahab when he'd had a bite or two.

"Yes?"

"We were struck by lightning, the two of us."

I stopped chewing, astonished.

"Lightning is a curious thing," he continued. "What I've been able to learn, in our own particular case, is that something like the finger of God came down and touched me and found its way over to thee. From there, it seems to have gone into the sand or out into the ether, leaving us twitching and drooling but alive somehow."

"Well," I said, "there's luck."

For the first time, just then, I noticed that Ahab was marked. A long, crooked shadow ran from his temple to his chest . . . no, to his hip, and all the way down to his ankle. Black and jagged and wicked looking, it swelled and blistered in places.

"Thou art scarred, too," he told me.

Startled, I surveyed my own skin and discovered identical blisters, an identical zig-zagging shadow.

"Lightning's handprint," I whispered.

He nodded.

The doorway darkened. The woman with the magic eyes appeared there.

"I am going to the village for water," she said. "If one of you accompanies me, it's more water and less work."

"I'll go," I said, wanting to be helpful. Wanting to do anything that made me less likely to be killed and eaten.

"We shall all go," said Ahab. "But let it wait awhile, until Pitch and I have fashioned ourselves some kind of clothing." He indicated the bundle of grass he had brought to the hut. "I don't mean to go about like Adam all the day long."

Magic Eyes seemed to understand and agree, so we sat down to see what we could make of the grasses. While we worked, Magic Eyes answered some questions for us, and our situation became less of a mystery.

We learned, firstly, that her name wasn't Magic Eyes. It was Tangi. Like this: TAHN-jee.

Secondly, we learned that most of the local people lived in a nearby town called Qool (pronounced "Kool"). The men we had encountered were warriors from this town. They had been on their way to make war on another settlement when the storm hit. Taking shelter, they had discovered us among the rocks.

"We're grateful not to have been eaten," I told Tangi and made a sign that, in some places, means "thank you."

She gave me a look like you give a child when it says something foolish and informed us that being struck by lightning was the reason we had been brought here, to Mama-o Lava.

"Mama—?" I said.

She waved her hand, indicating the hut and the other huts close by. "This place," she said, "away from the town. Mama-o Lava. It means 'apart.' You are too *oti* to go among the people."

"*Oti*?" asked Ahab.

Oti, Tangi explained, could be good or bad but was always powerful. A powerful work of art might be considered *oti*. That was good. Someone who raised healthy animals for food was *oti*. So was a warrior who killed a lot of enemies. *Oti* was something that accrued inside you like a kind of fire.

As with any fire, the right amount was useful, but too much could destroy you. If a warrior killed a really unusual number of enemies, for example, he might become so *oti* that people were afraid to live near him, and he might have to go make his home outside of town for a while.

"You," said Tangi, looking at Ahab and me, "are something else, called '*Oti-bei*.' It means something is powerful but in a frightening and unknown way. Powerful not like a warrior but like the earth itself. Like the sun and moon and the sea. Women must come and live at Mama-o Lava when they are in their monthly tides. And when they are pregnant. And when they are giving birth. You are here because lightning has touched you and let you live. Or it has killed you, and you have returned from the dead. Because of these things, the people in Qool want nothing to do with you. They won't harm you, but they don't want you walking around among them, either."

By the time she was finished with the explaining, and our skirts were complete, I was burning to ask Tangi why she, herself, lived at Mama-o Lava.

Ahab beat me to it.

"Thou must be *oti* as well," he ventured.

Tangi draped his skirt over his head. The other she handed to me. We stood, dressed, and followed her outside. A brief stop was made at her hut, where we procured several water buckets in the form of dried-out gourds, and we struck out down a narrow jungle path for town.

The town was about as far away as a strong man could throw a hammer. As villages go, Qool was well and sturdily built. Houses with wooden frames, expertly thatched, protected by hanging mats of woven grass. Some distance down the street was a hole surrounded with large black volcanic rocks, which I took to be the well, and beyond that a great longhouse, like an island edition of a Massachusetts church.

"Where is everybody?" I asked.

Not a single child played between the houses; not a single man or woman walked or worked or peered from windows.

But wait! Here came a long, thin, angry-looking fellow with a spear you could have run through five horses.

"Stop!" he told us, making faces, waving us off. "Go!"

"*O le a le mea etemana'oai*?" Ahab asked this person. "Which is it? Stop or go? Either way, we'll need water."

"Not today," the sentry answered. "When the fighting men return. Then you can come."

Tangi spat. "We'll get water at the river," she told us. "It's farther, but the stream will be fresh since the rain."

"*Leai*," said Ahab. "No."

The sentry and Tangi both scowled at him.

"No," he repeated in a particular voice I knew well, and you didn't have to be a close friend to understand that he wasn't going anywhere until he got what he'd come for.

Best to throw in with Ahab when he gets like that.

"No," I said, crossing my arms over my chest.

Tangi, with a good deal of eye rolling, turned to the sentry and made it plain that she wasn't going anywhere, either.

At this point, a second sentry came jogging up the street. No, not a sentry. Instead of a spear, he carried a tall, wonderfully carved staff festooned in feathers with a skull sitting at the top. His skin was a gallery of tattooed designs, and his eyes were both bright and cool, like ice melting in sunlight. A priest?

"Go," he said to us.

"Water," said Ahab.

The priest seemed unperturbed. Shrugging, he drew a line in the earth, representing, I decided, the perimeter of the town, said "Go" again, and turned around and walked away. The sentry followed him.

Immediately, I made as if to take a step forward (goddammit, I was thirsty!), but Ahab stopped me.

"Not until we're invited," he said.

So we stood there.

And stood there. And stood there. And stood there. And stood there.

I was not prepared, in my head or my body, for how long we stood. Few people would be, whether or not they had a humped shoulder and a bent spine already giving them hell.

After a time—and by "a time" I mean the full, long afternoon—I began to get the shakes.

I was on the verge of testing the waters of surrender, suggesting that we must have made our point to some degree, already. But no one wants to be the first to give way, least of all a New Englander.

So we stood.

Night came. The moon rose, and when it had gone halfway across the sky, Ahab cleared his throat and said, "John?"

"Yes, Charles?" (He *hates* that name. But I was pissed off and thought this might get under his skin.)

"John, look to our right, yonder, just where the trees begin, will you?"

I looked. I saw trees and shadows and moonlight. And . . . something else.

"What is it I'm supposed to see?" I asked.

"You don't see, I suppose, an old woman with a necklace made of sea-shells and white dots painted across her forehead?"

I looked harder. Whatever I saw, it was hazy.

"I'm not sure," I said.

"An old woman," he added, "with notably large eyes and seaweed in her hair?"

"Maybe," I said.

Tiny hairs stood up all over my body. What kind of unnatural business was this? Hallucinations, sparked by pain and fatigue? Maybe my brain was half asleep out of pure boredom.

Tangi said, "It's my mother."

"You see her?" asked Ahab urgently.

Tangi shook her head, saying, "No. But between the necklace and the seaweed, I know it must be her. She drowned in the sea five monsoons ago."

"I'm confused," said I, struggling to keep my voice steady. I looked away from the woman—the ghost?—but could still feel her cold, supernatural eyes upon me.

"It seems," Tangi said to us, "that the lightning has built a new kind of fire inside you by which you see things others cannot. It has happened before among the *oti-bei*."

Ahab digested this.

"Well," he said, "perhaps I also see, in the shadows between two huts yonder, a tall, thin man missing his head and a shorter man looking mauled and somewhat eaten, and, down near the well, a whole family who appear to be, well, *smoldering*—"

I saw the same. I tried *not* to, but no use.

"The dead," Tangi confirmed, making signs with her hands.

The rest of the night passed in relative silence save for the occasional hoots and screams in the jungle. Every now and then, Ahab and I would look to the left or right and see things that startled us.

A young man with one arm half gone, bloodless and pale. A middle-aged couple, mad with fever, gibbering nonsense at each other.

Squeezing my eyes shut, I tried to sleep standing up.

A geological age passed. Mountains rose and fell. Dawn came.

The fighting men returned and were welcomed.

Wherever they had been, and whatever they had done, they had been successful. They emerged from the woods at the far end of town and went straight to the well. Within seconds, the houses up and down the street erupted in shrieks and shouts and jumping and running and singing, and a thousand people emerged. Every one of them did their best to hug and touch the warriors, who looked as if they wanted a drink of water and a bed more than anything else.

Fueled by alcohol, the festival lasted all morning. Shouts turned to screams, songs turned into—well, screams. In short, it resembled any tavern district in any American city on any Saturday night.

I was thinking that now might be a good time to walk quietly back to Mama-o Lava and pursue our case tomorrow when heads were clearer all around, but just then the entire festival changed tone and lurched in our direction.

"Oh shit," said I.

The festival moved fast. In an instant, the people of Qool surrounded us, staring.

The warriors, at the forefront, looked familiar, being the same fellow-ship that had discovered us during the storm. They looked exceedingly tired and didn't seem moved to say much. It was the older men, women, and kids bubbling around them and behind them who seemed to provide the festival's energy, pointing and making faces, ridiculing my hump. They, in turn, were egged on by the priest and the sentry, who soon shoved their way to the front.

"Him," said the guard, pointing a finger at Ahab.

One of the soldiers, the tall, heavily decorated fellow Ahab had tried to communicate with days before, gave a tired sigh and said, "Him what?"

"The troublemaker. This is his idea. Standing here and not going away like we told them."

The soldier (their king? president? pope?) looked us over without saying anything.

"We're thirsty," I told him. "We're still thirsty."

The townspeople muttered darkly and shuffled in a way I didn't like.

Sure enough, someone threw a rock and hit me right in the hump. I gave a strangled grunt. Inwardly, I screamed.

I was going to shout a reminder that we were supposed to be holy and dreadful, but before I got the words out, Ahab spoke, employing his best Massachusetts Quaker voice.

"You men look unwell," he observed, aloud, to the leader.

It was true. They did.

The leader frowned, and, in a Quaker voice of his own, asked what that was supposed to mean.

"Just that," said Ahab. "You've all worked hard, and fought hard, and been very strong. But you feel sleepy and sick, don't you? It's a hundred degrees out, but two or three of you have the shivers, like a sickness is on you."

The tall man shrugged, saying, "It's always that way, after a battle. Besides, Koni-Goloi and Ongeibi have been killed, which is depressing. How else should we feel?"

Ahab said he was sorry to hear about their dead friends. "But that's not what makes thee sick."

He pointed at a number of the warriors, each in turn.

"Thee, thee, thee, thee, thee, and thee," he said (this included the leader), "killed at least one man in the fighting. Yes?"

"How do you know?" asked the leader. "And what difference does it make?"

"Because," said Ahab, "the men thou hast killed are standing behind you, trying to strangle you with their bare, dead hands."

It was true. Now that Ahab mentioned it, I saw them, too. This supernatural sight we'd acquired was stronger in him, it seemed. That was Ahab for you. He was magnified, as if three or four extra souls were stuffed inside him.

The warriors silently considered what he'd told them. They looked doubtful.

Tangi said, "It's no trick. He can see. They both can. They saw my mother last night. It's part of their *boa*." (*Boa* means *soul*. It's a great word because it also means *heart*, *pecker*, and *pussy*.)

They ignored her.

Ahab offered specifics. "*You*," he said, pointing, "killed a man with a cassowary bird tattooed on his chest. *You* killed *three* men. Congratulations. One of them wore a shark tooth on a string around his neck—"

Most of the townspeople retreated down the street, making nervous signs.

The warriors looked the way you might look if someone had just revealed that you were covered with invisible spiders.

"King Hota," said the priest, stepping forward, "I can make them go away."

King Hota said, "That would be great, Io Io, especially if you can manage it quickly."

Io Io sank to his knees, raised his staff over his head, and muttered. Whatever he was doing—at first, at least—was almost silent, almost motionless. It was quite impressive, except that, as time passed, it didn't seem to be working.

"He doesn't see them," Ahab said in a low voice.

"I could have told you that," Tangi said dryly.

"I think," said Ahab, "that the matter is a simple misunderstanding."

"Meaning?" said I.

"They don't know they're dead."

And with that, he stepped forward and pointed into the face of the first dead spirit on the right, a slender fellow with green stripes across his face and part of a spear lodged in his throat.

"*Faanoanoatele*," he said, gently enough. "I'm sorry, but thou hast been killed. Off to *laueleele o le oti*, the Land of the Dead, with thee!"

The dead man looked startled. Then he nodded, as if this explained a thing or two. He vanished into the trees, scratching at his neck. Instantly, the local hero he'd been tormenting stood up straight and seemed improved.

"Well and good!" said the king. "My turn!"

"Now, just a damn m-minute—" stammered the priest.

Still impatient, still thirsty, Ahab worked his way down the line, pointing and speaking sternly, not unlike a schoolmaster. One by one the ghosts limped away, fading.

King Hota clapped Ahab on his shoulder and me—*ow!*—on my hump, saying, "Get what you need from the well. Yimaa and Bako"—he indicated two of his warriors—"will go with you to make sure you're not bothered. Then go home. Soon, we'll talk more."

"Thank you," said we.

Ahab turned to say something to Io Io, but the priest spoke up first. What he said didn't take long. He turned and sped off down the street, gesturing as he went.

"I thought only Nantucket sailors had a word for that," said I, surprised.

"We'll hear more from him, too," said Ahab. "Thou canst be sure. Mind your stern."

"Water," said Tangi, always focused. "Go."

Back at Mama-o Lava, Tangi assigned me a hut.

"That's *my* hut," said Ahab.

"You share for now. These others are occupied." And she pointed around to each of the houses, saying, "Pregnant woman, pregnant woman, woman about to give birth, old dying man, two sisters in their monthly tides, pregnant woman, pregnant woman—"

Ahab and I shuffled into our shared home, falling-down tired but at least rehydrated.

It wasn't an uncomfortable lodging. A thick grass mat on the floor is plenty of mattress, if you're used to ship's accommodations.

Later that night, I told Ahab, "Our hut, here, is nice enough, but we'll need a plan that will see us home."

He didn't answer right away. Twilight deepened into dark.

"They have canoes," he said. "Great, long war canoes, and outriggers for fishing. We'll stay long enough to earn one of these or else build our own. We'll sail out to the whaling grounds with enough food to keep a village for a week. That should see us rescued."

"Suits me," said I.

"Good," he answered. "Now, if thee don't mind, Pitch, I'll close my eyes and try for sleep. There's a dead man standing in the door, yonder, missing one eye, looking at us with the other."

So there was. Lovely.

We slept.

In our first days on the island, Ahab and I spent a lot of time gathering food. We were surprised at how weak we'd gotten.

We began by searching the ground for fallen fruit and wild berries. Soon enough, though, we were able to climb into the trees after coconuts, whose milk refreshed us and brought color back to our cheeks. Indeed, the island seemed to suit Ahab particularly well. His eyes sharpened. He grew strong and supple like a thing carved out of green wood.

The lightning, as we'd been told, had struck my companion first. So it was no great surprise, as time passed, that my part of the new fire turned to ash. I saw the dead spirits less and less, until I could only see them now and then, in a certain kind of moonlight. In Ahab, on the other hand, the fire quickened like a lamp that's been turned up.

"They're everywhere, John," he complained. "Even out on the lagoon, by the razor coral."

At first, the supernatural vision frightened him, and he developed a twitch in his eye, but it wasn't long before it turned to our advantage.

Turned into a job, to be exact.

It came in the form of a man and a woman—youngish, married, wearing identical pink stone necklaces—who walked into Mama-o Lava one morning, looking nervous.

"Tall white man!" they called out.

The pregnant women and the monthly women and Tangi all poked their heads out to see what was going on. Ahab, rubbing his eyes and adjusting his skirt, sallied out to meet them.

"Thou callest?" he asked.

You could tell the couple didn't want to be there. They kept looking around as if expecting to find dark forces sneaking up on them.

What they wanted was for Ahab to contact the man's dead brother and ask where he had hidden his mattock.

Ahab raised an eyebrow but said nothing.

It was, they explained, an especially powerful mattock with which the brother had plowed ten seasons of successful *taro* crops. The brother had stashed it somewhere secret, and then he had stepped on a stonefish and died.

Ahab didn't know what to say or do, but the problem took care of itself.

The brother came limping out of the trees on his poisoned foot, saying, "I suppose they're asking about the mattock."

Ahab said that they were, indeed.

"Tepi has it," said the brother. "I loaned it to him. Tell him I said to give it back."

Ahab relayed the message. The couple thanked him and left. That afternoon, the man returned and left a pile of fresh breadfruit outside our door.

"Well," said Ahab, regarding this treasure. "Hmmm."

An old woman came walking up just then.

"My sister died in her sleep last year," she said to Ahab. "Can you tell her I'm sorry I stole her *banyiki* recipe?"

"We might be on to something," Ahab mused, and he was right.

The end of the first week had brought us a fortune in dried pork, bananas, and breadfruit. Our favorite was an entire scraped and tanned pig skin, from which we added to our wardrobe. As time passed, Ahab's wealth grew to include necklaces of stone, shell, coral, and animal bone. As our hair grew, we learned to tie it up in ponytails with leather cords.

"We're a couple of handsome fellows again, Pitch," said he.

"If you like that kind of thing," said I with a great big hunchbacked shrug.

Time did what time does.

A rainy season came and went. A great festival was celebrated, in which the men danced in elaborate costumes made to resemble leaves. They whirled and leaped as if blown by the wind, celebrating growth and food and abundance. The dance was like an engine; it made good things happen. The dance and the festival were *oti*.

As the rains diminished and the winds shifted, Ahab and I fell into conversation about the boat we planned to build, but it changed into a conversation about the best way to make a new roof for the hut, which had leaked during the monsoons. So the roof was improved, and the boat set aside for a season.

Ahab talked to the dead. This was a good thing and a bad thing. Good, because it brought us food. Bad, because, like a wave that rolls and builds, it brought more ghosts to our door.

"Don't sit there," he would say to me. "A dead man with one eye is sitting there, complaining to me about his wife, who has remarried," or "Don't eat that. There's already someone trying to eat it."

It was no surprise that Ahab's business success displeased Io Io, the priest. He gave us the dead eye whenever we crossed paths, which was often.

"Tangi," Ahab told me, "says he bears watching. She has seen him whispering in Hota's ear and making signs in the air. Signs that mean 'Tall White Man' and 'The Man Who Carries a Hill Around On His Back.'" (These were our island names. They sounded better if you didn't translate them.)

A month after we arrived, King Hota gathered the warriors for a raid. The war canoes were dragged out and cleansed of spiders. Spears were sharpened. The dead were consulted.

Ahab and I presented ourselves for duty.

"We have fought pirates," I told Fuum, the first warrior.

"I have hunted and fought alongside the Shawnee," Ahab told him.

Fuum looked impressed, and I was sure he was going to let us join the raid, until Io Io the priest arrived and shook his long, tattooed finger at us.

"*Leai!*" he spat. "No! *Oti-bei!*"

Fuum gave us an apologetic look but shrugged as if to say the decision was out of his hands.

Ahab cursed all the way home (good, solid Quaker curses, too).

"Can you blame him?" I asked. "I'll bet you've taken up half of his business."

"Tangi says it's his own fault," he growled, "for not being a particularly good priest."

Tangi reminded Ahab that night that he would never be fully accepted by the priest or anyone else.

"*Yo-valloo-va,*" she told him. "You are not from this island, not from this earth."

It didn't sit well with him, and, indeed, wasn't the first time he'd been cast as an outsider. Nantucket itself, where he'd owned a house for ten years, still scorned him as a mainlander. A native-born innkeeper had once explained this to him, saying, "If a cat crawls into an oven, that doesn't make her a biscuit."

Put together with his having been orphaned as a baby, I wondered if Ahab didn't consider himself cursed with a certain unrooted quality. At home on the sea and nowhere else.

As for me, I was for getting home. Soon, maybe, I'd raise the issue of building our boat again. For now, Ahab was too busy stewing in his own resentment.

"I don't know how she comes to tell me where I do or don't belong," he complained. "She hath outcast issues of her own."

We still didn't know why Tangi didn't live in the village. If you asked, she would get an eerie, distant look in her eye and slip away. I thought she might be more forthcoming after she and Ahab started eating breakfast together every day, but she didn't.

Before the raiders hit the warpath, they had one hell of a party down at the longhouse. (I had been right, I would learn, in comparing the longhouse to a church. As it turned out, I might also have compared it to an opium den, an art gallery, a theater, a poker parlor, and a haunted house.) Even at Mama-o Lava, we could hear shouts and songs and speeches, growing wilder by the hour. At first, with nothing better to do, Ahab and I sat around drinking *wojo* juice and feeling pouty and left out. As the howls and prayers grew louder, though, we thought maybe we had the best of it right where we were. Again, I found myself satisfied with being kept on the fringes of things. My gravity pulled from homeward, whether that home was Nantucket or a whaling ship. Ahab, though he said nothing, watched the fires in the village with frustrated longing. He sat leaning that way as if the ritual madness were pulling at him with invisible hooks.

Near dawn, when the ritual madness seemed to have subsided, Ahab and I had just about decided we might get some sleep when a bizarre figure appeared in our door, wearing an enormous mask in the form of a bird. No, a pig. Hard to tell.

"Hi," said this figure, weaving.

King Hota.

We stood and welcomed him and invited him to be seated on the floor-mat. The mask fell to one side, leaving Hota blinking at us with bleary, benevolent eyes.

"I'm sorry you can't go on the raid," he told us. "I came up here to tell you that."

We appreciated this and told him so.

"At the same time," he said—sobering a bit, I thought—"there's another reason. It's important."

He looked us in the eyes to see if we were listening. We were.

"Tell you a story," he said, "about the reason we have a priest, even if this particular priest is *weeloo*. Silly. And difficult."

There was a long silence. I was about to give him a shake and see if he had fallen asleep when he came back to life and waved his hands around in a storytelling kind of way.

"A long time ago," he said, "like waaaaaaaay long ago when everything was new, all the animals were just like people and could talk and everything. They talked about the new things that were going on, like the ocean and the stars and rain and day and night. One of the things that really got their attention was when the volcano would go off, because that's always impressive. Right? Have you ever seen a volcano go off?"

"No," said we.

"Well, it's impressive. So it occurs to all the animals that there are massive, important things going on not just in the sky and in the ocean but down in the earth, too. So they decide they're all going to go up on the volcano and talk to the fire god and get him to tell them the secrets of the earth. So all the animals go on this big hike up the mountain, all except . . . guess who."

"Man," said Ahab and I, simultaneously.

"Why?" asked King Hota.

"Because he's lazy," guessed Ahab.

"You've heard this before," said the king, disappointed.

"I've heard lots of stories," Ahab told him. "The men are always lazy. Lazier than the women, anyway."

Hota nodded, saying, "That's true. Well, so all the other, nonlazy animals go up the volcano and look down and tell the fire god they want to know the secrets of the earth. And the fire god is all fiery and loud, right, but he's also surprisingly agreeable. And he says, 'Are you sure?' and they all say, 'Yes!' Which anyone who knows anything knows this is the part where you should be suspicious and ask, 'What's the catch?' but the world was so new, they didn't know that yet. So the volcano god says, 'Okay!' and tells the animals everything they want to know, but it's so loud and explosive and huge that it blows the animals' minds and sends them all flying off into the forests and oceans and everything, and the animals are so astonished they forget how to speak. So ever since then, the animals know the secrets of the earth but can't say what they are or discuss them with anybody. Meanwhile, here's lazy old Man, talking a mile a minute, even though he has no idea what the fire god said to the beasts."

He got quiet again, and this time he *had* fallen asleep. I poked him.

"That's why we have Io Io," he yawned, standing, "and priests in general. We have to figure out the really deep stuff that the animals just automatically know. We're so full of words, right, that we forget—"

He trailed off and just waved his hand around.

"So we give Io Io some room. Him, and priests in general."

I handed him his gigantic mask, which he examined with puzzlement.

"Is this thing supposed to be a bird or a pig?" he asked, making his way out the door. "See, that's what I'm talking about. That's something an animal would know without asking. Or a priest would know, maybe, and *him* you can talk to."

He turned around, just before disappearing among the trees, and fixed Ahab with a clear, cold-sober eye.

"You're a priest, too, you know," he said.

Ahab didn't answer, which seemed an intelligent move.

The warriors were gone for five days, and on the sixth day they came home (except for Fuum, who was killed) triumphant, carrying the skull of the enemy king. This was considered a great prize; it was promptly boiled, painted, and given its own hut at Mama-o Lava. Ahab made note of enemy ghosts hanging around the warriors and shooed them away.

Io Io glared at us and went around whispering in ears.

The war party had also been a hunting party, it seemed. A huge wild sow had been killed and helped provide for the feast. Yimma brought me two of her children, a boy piglet and a girl piglet.

"You can start a family!" he laughed. Others laughed, too, but I took the piglets back to Mama-o Lava and secured them in the hut while I built a fence and foraged for roots. When I had fashioned a gate, I let my pigs, Adam and Eve, out into my bamboo corral, and just like that, I was a pig farmer.

A year passed. New fruit bloomed and dropped. Eve grew big and pregnant. Soon enough, I would have a herd, which meant meat and wealth.

When Cain and Abel and Jim and Peter and Libby and Mary and Jeanette and Molly and Forthright and Gregory and Michael and Penelope were born, I set Michael and Molly aside to breed and branded the rest for market, as soon as they should have grown and gotten fat. One of them, Forthright, I had to set free for fear he would eat his brothers and sisters. How peculiar, I thought, the different kinds of spirits that get into things, human, animal, and otherwise. Here was a pig born of the same litter as these others, yet born with a fire and a hunger and a hate inside him. Born, too, with a curious birthmark: an entire leg colored red, as if he'd stepped in blood. Anyhow, off went Forthright to seek his fortune in the jungle.

All of this was very comfortable, and this made me wary. I visited Ahab in his hut—which was Tangi's hut, too, now—and told him I was surprised to find us still living on the island and not walking the streets of Nantucket.

I found him busily smoking a pipeful of *pwavva* leaves, which produced more smoke than a Boston warehouse fire. As he considered his answer, the entire hut became obscured in a dark, hovering cloud. Ahab enjoyed this property of the leaves, saying it kept ghosts away when he didn't wish to be pestered, or at least rendered them invisible.

"I *had* noticed," he said, from somewhere in this haze, "that work on our canoe has gone slowly."

"Indeed," said I, "for it hasn't yet begun."

"That's so," he said. "Well, let's make a start tomorrow, then? Or next week, perhaps."

As we talked, the *pwavva* smoke worked on our brains, and I left without completely understanding what we had agreed to undertake.

So nothing was undertaken.

The moon turned through her phases.

More seasons came and went. Dry seasons and rainy seasons, alternating like tides.

Among the ordinary days and hours came occasional wonders, like the great two-headed fish caught by Nwai, the *pwavva* farmer. Like the day the river flowed backward for an hour. Like the vast wave of hermit crabs that rose from the sea on the eastern coast, swarmed through the town, and vanished into the surf on the western side, one clear and otherwise lovely spring day.

"Given enough time," Ahab observed once, smoking his *pwavva* pipe, "I suppose *everything* happens at least once."

I married a widow named Hhhyeai and raised so many pigs that they wouldn't let me live in Mama-o Lava anymore. I found myself transplanted onto a green patch amid other farmers. I began to feel my previous life fading, drifting out of reach. Sometimes this distressed me, sometimes not.

I got in the habit of borrowing one of the fishing outriggers and paddling out into the lagoon at night. When the moon was down, I had discovered, the calm waters so clearly reflected the stars in their fiery billions that I easily lost my bearings between heaven and earth and fell hypnotized by the illusion of floating between the planets as on an ocean between islands.

One night, as I drifted thus, the universe spoke to me in a deep, relaxed tone, saying, "We're of the same mind, I see, friend Pitch."

To my port side, I discerned the tall figure of King Hota in an outrigger of his own.

"The stars," I said.

"I know," he quietly answered.

Our canoes, as canoes near to each other in still water do, drew together. After a time, he spoke again.

"I've wondered, Pitch, what it is that gives you this shape you live in." I could see him making a hump with his shoulder. "Were you born with it? Does it mean something?"

I have never minded questions about my hump, if they are not rudely put. So I found myself telling him about the meningitis I'd suffered, and survived, as a child.

"I don't know that it means anything," I said. "It's just something that happens. Just another detail in a big universe."

"Don't they say God is in the details?" asked King Hota. "My mother's father, my grandfather Nakko, used to say there was nothing to know that wasn't already known by his foot or his penis."

I said that I thought Nakko might have underestimated how much there was to know.

"Indeed," I said, "the more I learn, the more I seem surrounded by mysteries."

Hota gave the universe a long, significant stare, sighing, "Yes."

"Not like that," I said. "It's mostly ordinary things. Why do *puio* berries give me a rash? Why do my pigs like to eat pork? My hair gets less curly every year. Why?"

"Why indeed," said Hota, still watching the universe.

"And what happened to Tangi," I wondered, "that she has to stay in a hut at Mama-o Lava when she is neither bearing a child, nor has her tides, nor is dying?"

If it weren't for Tangi, I sometimes thought but never said, we would long ago have built our boat.

Hota hung his head sadly. "Tangi," he said simply.

One of the things you learn, if you live long enough, is that the best way to find the answer to something, half the time, is to just be quiet and wait and not bother people with more questions.

I waited long enough for the stars to wheel clockwise a degree or two.

"Tangi," he said, "was once married to a fisherman named Lo Mariiarii. An unremarkable man with one ear bigger than the other. One night he dreamed that he had been eaten by a tiger shark. It was a terrible dream, a powerful dream. So bad and powerful, in fact, that Io Io demanded that he move out to Mama-o Lava for a time. Before he could move his things, though, a tiger shark actually *did* eat him. Very strange and *oti* and sad."

"Sad," I repeated.

"He left Tangi behind with a daughter, a girl they called Fweii. One day, Tangi went swimming in the lagoon with her mother and daughter, and the child was caught in the undertow and pulled out through the reef.

"Tangi and her mother were braver than any five warriors; they swam into the rip and were shot out into the deep water, where they followed the child down into the blue.

"But the sea wouldn't give her up. Down and down went Fweii, and they dove after her kicking hard.

"Neither Fweii nor her grandmother came back up. The waves rolled Tangi ashore a week later. My own daughter, Maia, found her."

The stars turned.

"A week," I whispered, awed. "*Oti* or not, how could a person live through such a thing?"

The king looked at me strangely, as if I had confirmed some sort of suspicion.

"She didn't, of course," he said, and paddled softly away, leaving me staring and drifting and barely daring to breathe.

↓

A week later, a terrible, bloodthirsty wild boar appeared like Grendel out of the jungle. Tusks like swords, bigger around than a steam engine, he burst through the tree line and killed a banana farmer then gored and trampled his neighbor, a pig farmer, and ate that season's piglets. Io Io declared that this was obviously an *oti*-pig, with mad eyes and an evil red leg, who would not stop or go away until measures were taken.

With my head hanging, I went to King Hota when these calamities became known and told him about my piglet, Forthright. "Tis my fault," I said.

He gave me a hard look and said, "Since you bred the thing, it's yours to kill. Maybe only an *oti* can kill it."

Just this once, it was decided, Ahab and I could hunt. *Lots* of hunters would go, after they'd been properly anointed and subject to powerful, protective rituals.

Ahab and I walked down the main thoroughfare, past the well (for the first time), to the enormous longhouse where the men met to tell stories, and make judgments, and work magic. Longer than five whaling ships, taller at its open end than six giraffes stacked on top of each other, the longhouse, inside, was a wonder. Inside, shields and spears and ornaments of all kinds hung from great beams and wide columns carved from whole trees. Masks peered from everywhere. Indeed, when the hunt had gathered inside, Io Io immediately commanded us to take masks and wear them until either the boar was killed or the boar killed us.

I chose a mask with huge, spiraling eyes and actual boar tusks sticking out like horns.

Ahab chose a mask that was like a fire made of wood, bright orange, with eyes like—

"*Leai!*" shouted the priest, leaping between hunters, landing squarely in front of Ahab. "No! For you, I have chosen already."

He jerked the fire mask from Ahab's hands and thrust another at him. A shape like a crescent moon with nothing in it but eyes, as if it were the face of night, or a ghost.

Everyone gasped.

"The Mask of Va-i-Fafo!" they murmured. "The Mask of Outer Space!"

"Given to the island people by the sky people!" sang Io Io, hands raised, eyes spinning. "It can only be worn by a hunter whose vision and heart are clear and true!"

"Great," I muttered.

But all around me they chattered in awed tones. "For a bad soul or even an ordinary soul to wear it means *oti ma seoli*! Death and hell!" And they made signs and kept their distance.

Ahab took the mask and strapped it on, saying, "God's left thumb! There's work to do! What else hast thou, priest?"

When he didn't fall down dead, most of the hunters shrugged and waited for the next wonder to happen.

Io Io, seemingly unfazed, spoke over us and prayed over us and told stories over us all through one night and part of a morning. Then we tore into a hearty breakfast of raw pork and erupted from the house like a volcano had gone off, screaming our way through town, through some trees, down the beach, and back into the trees. Headed away from the village, led by Aahui, the first hunter. Aahui had killed a tiger shark, once, with a knife made from the beak of a cassowary, and had been sent three times to live at Mama-o Lava until his power subsided.

Right behind Aahui ran Ahab.

I had witnessed my friend in the throes of a hundred whale hunts. I had lived with him among the Shawnee and seen him chase elk on foot, but I'd never seen him like this. He carried his borrowed spear high overhead, as if it were a wing he meant to follow into the air and cruise the jungle canopy like a mad and deadly eagle. His face I could only imagine, hidden behind the moon mask.

Quickly enough, Aahui called for the hunt to slow down, and the reason was me, with my uniquely shaped self, not adapted to running through jungles for hours. It was decided the hunt would rest, and maybe pick some breadfruit for lunch, until I had quite caught my breath.

"There's some bananas, too," said Aahui, dropping his shield, planting his spear in the ground, "just there, and if anyone has to take a piss, there's a nice cheese tree—"

Pow! The giant boar blasted out of the underbrush and tore Aahui wide open. It spilled his guts and trampled him like a ripe squash. All in one sudden, hellish moment.

Grunt! Squeal! The monster scattered the other hunters like ninepins and raced straight for me.

It mowed me to the ground and trampled me. My shield got in between us, somehow, so I wasn't pierced. I *was* half crushed, though, and felt that my shoulder and spine would snap in two.

"Pig!" someone shouted.

The pig had knocked Ahab aside in the first rush, he being so close behind poor Aahui, but he had sprung up and now hailed the monster through that weird mask of his.

"*Yaaaaa!*" he bellowed. "*Pig pigpigpigpig! Yaaaa!*"

But the pig wanted *me*. Did he really remember me? And what, in particular, had I done to him, really, except set him free? It wasn't fair, and I told him so.

My shield cracked. My spine gave a *pop*, and—

Ahab charged, spear raised high, screaming. For an instant, the hunters later said, it seemed he would have the monster straight up the bunghole, but at the last moment the beast wheeled around, only to take Ahab's spear right in the throat.

"*Bwaaaaaaaaaaaaaaaaaaaaah!*" roared Ahab, leaning into the blow, roaring in the pig's face.

The rest of the hunt gave a ferocious cheer.

But with a wild squeal, the dying monster heaved itself halfway up the spear. Vomiting blood, it heaved again, and again, fighting its way up to Ahab, who waited behind his white mask.

Ahab steeled himself to take whatever wounds the beast was able to give. "*Squeeeeeeeeeeeeeeeeeeeeeeeeeeeeeeeeeeeeeeee!*" said the beast, lunging.

"*Bwaaaaaaaaaaaaaaaaaaaaaaaaaaaaaaaaaaaaaaah!*" screamed Ahab.

The pig charged all the way up the spear, broke a tusk off in Ahab's shoulder, and died an explosive, deafening, puking death right on top of him.

The rest of us jumped in upon the instant, rolling the boar off Ahab, who lay bleeding and gasping and struggling to untie his mask.

Bare-faced, he looked as I had imagined him: wild-eyed, teeth bared, and, at the moment, half blind with terror.

"Jesus Christ!" he shuddered, gulping for air, groping at the tusk planted in his flesh.

"You're supposed to *throw* the spear," someone told him.

He strained to pull the tusk loose, but it wasn't ready to come, yet. He collapsed again, wheezing.

"*Otaota o tagata!*" cried the hunters. "Shit!"

Their voices had a tone I didn't like, and in an instant I saw why . . . Ahab's face was demon red and swelling like a wineskin.

"*Otaota a tagata!*" the hunters repeated. "Death and hell!"

Making magic signs like crazy, they leaped away. Those who had touched Ahab or the dreaded mask rubbed their hands in the earth.

Out of nowhere, suddenly, Io Io was among us.

"Haven't I told you?" he asked, shoving his way through the hunters as they backed away, standing over Ahab (who began to look as if he might be having trouble breathing), pointing down with a thin, accusing finger. "Haven't I said it? When the two-headed fish was caught? When the plague of crabs came? Haven't I said it a hundred times: there is a bad spirit among us, and it's pretty obvious who?"

"He has said it," the hunters admitted. "I've heard him."

They marveled at how quickly the curse of the mask was turning Ahab into something like a melon. Before long, he would burst, surely. He was making strangled noises now, sounding ironically pig-like.

I picked up the mask, to everyone's horror, and turned it over in my hands. With my thumbnail, I scraped at some yellow muck that had dried onto the polished wood.

"*Sese*," I said. "Bullshit. Someone's rubbed *puio* berries all over this thing. Give me water."

Nobody moved.

Io Io, as it happened, had a nice fat water gourd lashed to his waist. I snatched it up, emptied it over Ahab's face, and rubbed it around with the leather hem of my pigskin skirt.

When his breathing quieted some and the swelling abated, a few of the bolder hunters offered their water, too. As the minutes passed, he looked less and less cursed, and the hunters began muttering again and giving Io Io the dead eye. It wasn't in them, however, to lay hands on their priest or even say anything about him that wasn't nice.

"Well," he began, "it certainly *seemed* as if—"

No one I have ever known, then or since, bounces back like Ahab. One moment he was sitting up and catching his breath, the next he was a blur. He was up. There was something like a storm of arms and legs and evil words, and Ahab had Io Io over his shoulder.

He marched him straight back to town, crashing through the jungle, not bothering with the trail, and we followed on his heels, making dark noises in our throats. Straight as the crow flies, through the river and down the twilight street Ahab carried him, cuffing him in the mouth when he tried to say anything, till he reached the open plaza in front of the longhouse, and, with bared teeth and a wild cry, threw the priest down the well.

"Thou wouldst think," Ahab said at the feast that followed, "someone might have told me how to use the spear."

"You'd think a whaler would know something like that," they teased him.

But they toasted him, too. They were in awe of what he had done—with both pig and priest—just as they'd been in awe of Aahui when he killed the shark. They told a hundred stories like this, sitting in the longhouse after the hunt, eating pig meat by firelight, with an orchestra drumming in the background. Drinking something heady from the painted skull of the enemy king, freed from its hut at Mama-o Lava for this one night. Stories of awe about the time Jitwaa caught a giant octopus with a hoop (a child's toy) and a basket of dried banana leaves. The time Fuum and his twin brother, Muuf, had dropped from a tree onto the back of a giant cassowary (like, a cassowary the size of a house) and ridden it up and down the island and over the sea and back before managing to strangle it with a *looki* vine. And that was nothing, if you remembered the time Fuum stopped the volcano from erupting by making a huge plug out of nothing but sour milk, and—

The stories waxed taller the more the skull got passed around.

Right in the middle of all this, just when I was saying that the second moon was brighter and more beautiful than her sister, three of the younger men marched in, carrying a platter shaped from one long, black rock. On the platter was more pork, arranged in neatly cut filets on a bed of banana leaves, sprinkled with *iijikii* petals.

Except it wasn't pork.

"Aahui," said Ahab.

The others nodded, whispering, "Aahui."

Everyone reached in and took some. *Almost* everyone. I couldn't.

Ahab, however, gave the meat a long, big-eyed stare, took one of the filets in his hands, raised it toward the rafters like a Presbyterian does an offering, and ate every bite with solemn relish.

The very atmosphere throbbed, I thought. Strong drink will do that. I felt the souls of both the living and the dead around me. As the (blurry) twin moons rose higher and burned brighter, they surrounded us, singing their hollow songs. Even Aahui was there, shuffling and fingering his broken bones, trying to be a good sport.

Everything happens, given time.

More seasons, more tides, would rise and ebb. More pigs and children. In time, the volcano would gush fire. Wonders would appear, like the monsoon that rained fish and a comet and a great wave. One day, too, British explorers with guns would come ashore and drag Ahab and me—fighting and screaming—back to that other world.

But those things, those seasons, were far away.

On this night, we raced to the beach and swam across the starry lagoon, all the way out to the reef. We body-surfed waves in the dark, now and then taking wounds on the razor coral, daring the undertow and the mighty waves and sharks.

There was Ahab in the midst of it, rising atop one shining, breaking wave, howling up at the moons with all his might, bleeding from his shoulder, eyes full of raw joy, and I knew he had gone someplace he could never quite come back from.

We came ashore laughing, and much of the village met us on the white sand. Children and mothers and wives and old women, and the king and his queen and his other queen. Even the old, practical men joined us, having fished the priest out of the well. The wildness tightened into a certain kind of quiet you hear sometimes, a kind of music.

Tangi met Ahab in the knee-deep surf. She stood on tiptoe, moonlight shining through her, and pressed her forehead to his.

Hhhyeai met me on the sand and kissed me and said how brave I was and how strong, hunting monsters and carrying a hill around on my back.

"*Alofa*," I said, which means *love*.

She moved against me and said, "*Pao-weiia-pao*," which means something that's none of your business.

MICHAEL POORE is the author of the novels *Reincarnation Blues* and *Up Jumps the Devil*. His short work has appeared in numerous magazines and anthologies, including *The Year's Best Science Fiction* and *The Best American Nonrequired Reading 2012*. He lives with his wife, poet Janine Harrison, and daughter, Jianna, in Highland, Indiana.

5

Huck and Hominy: A Legend

Corey Mesler

Badly missing someone depopulates a world.
—Alexander Theroux

It is necessary to cross the bridges
and to reach the black murmur,
so that the perfume of lungs strike our temples
with its suit of warm pineapple.
—Federico Garcia Lorca

Dear Gumboots,
Yesterday evening at sunset the river must have been on fire the color
of the bars and buildings purred so. It was still so hot even after the sun
went down and the air seemed to be full of electricity and water as if such
a thing were possible, the river was a real presence on the street last night
I know you know what I mean. I know you remember. It was a reminder as
if I needed one that you were not here and it made me remember similar
nights when the weather would carry us out into the street with a drink or

a rib or such in our hands and we would stroll westward among the lively and life was so full of possibilities, I know you felt that too.

What's it like in Cincinnati, I can't even imagine. Is there music there? Is there colored folk? Do you like the job you took with the paper company, do they treat you nice?

At the club things are hot, so hot they hired a new girl named Callie. She's a stripper not just a waitress like myself and she is luscious and I guess I wish you could see her appreciator that you are of the feminine graces. She has skin like a Mississippi milkshake and the men fairly give up their seed when she first steps onto the runway. Mr. Burro I reckon likes her act and the money she is bringing our way.

This weekend you know is Cotton Makers and we're gussying up for that and putting on extra help and a few more guns and made a few deals on cut-rate booze and I don't know if we'll be ready or not. I don't think so but I feel that way every year and it works out all right.

Except this year you're not here.

Oh, Huck. I don't know about this. I'm trying to be good like you asked and talk of other things, just bringing you news off the street, just making my life appear normal or something. It ain't working.

You know I don't understand this "trial separation" thing, I don't follow. Mama said you were too modern with all that schooling and stuff and that psychology falala. Does absence really make the heart grow fonder, I don't think so. My heart hurts I mean it literally hurts like my accelerator's stuck. And I can't sleep.

I'm gonna have to close this before I get too carried away. I'm not pressuring you or anything, I'm fine really. I miss you is all and I know we'll get through this and you'll be back here as soon as soon. Mr. Burro said you could have your old job back anytime.

Give my love to your cousin Alligator.

yours and you know it

Hominy

Dear Honey-Hominy,

Oh you know I miss you too, Sweetcakes. I can't describe to you the world inside my head or make it any clearer but I know I just KNOW that this is for the best. Bear with me. You know I love you.

The job at Cuttermeyer's is a good job and has large chances for a young man to improve himself and Mr. Cuttermeyer has his eye on me I think I can tell already. He tipped his hat my way this morning and all I was doing was tying up stacks of boxes. A man who can get attention tying boxes is a man bound for the good life is the way I'm looking at that.

Cuttermeyer's daughter Laurie works here, well in the office. Short butt-y little white woman with the requisite turned-up nose and small spray of freckles and a mop of black curls, athletic legs all thigh and muscle and nothing on the top, not like you baby. Ohh I miss those amplenesses. And Laurie Cuttermeyer herself came down yesterday and smiled my way and said to the other men there so that her daddy and everyone could hear, "We should all work as hard as Huck here and maybe we wouldn't be heading for insolvency."

Well it made me proud and no doubt. If this works out for me here, well, I can't say now, but we'll have to see.

Glad to hear the club is doing well. I miss the boys and the strip shows and that lowdown house sound the BamBams concocted. I miss my drink, my Rub of the Brush. I miss Mississippi Sam Peeps and his steel doing "I Used to Be Black but I Lost the Knack."

Mostly I miss you and your cocoa thighs and your nipples like grapes and the way you say "oh heavenly host" and squinch your eyes up tight when you coming.

This gonna work out, Honey. We were getting stale together, going nowhere, stuck inside of Memphis and weighed down by the heat and the blood in our eyes. This resting time is gonna be the cure. Count on me.

Alligator sends his love back at you.

I'm your sugar-man.

love you betcha

Huck

Dear Huck Honey,

It was so good to get your letter and the reassurance and I read that letter three times and then took it to bed with me and in the morning read it one more time. My new friend Callie (did I tell you about her, she works at the club now?) came over and I read the letter to her and she's all cynical and all but she allowed as to how you sounded like a good man underneath.

The Jubilee was as crazy as ever and I didn't get to bed that night or none the next day until 2 in the afternoon but Mr. Burro said I was the backbone of the business and gave me an extra twenty for the sweat of it. We flat ran out of booze about midmorning and started selling the hootch

Old Riverbones makes in his flatboat and that went over well and all told on Beale only a half dozen negroes died in gunfights and elsewise. Not a bad year overall.

One crazy black man from Shaw Miss. got out into the middle of the street about midnight and fired his revolver into the air straight toward heaven and the bullet went straight up and came straight back down and pierced his skullcap and he's dead.

The crowds on the street that night were overwelling and it was a variable sea of black and everybody was there, Red Rolly, Bertah from Biloxi, Arty Shaw, Wild Bill Latura, Chuck the Knife, Axle Concertina, Styx, Sam, all the women you ever bedded, your cousin Lampedusa, the Greenville Gang, and that Loup Garou from the Clubs, skulking around, and it was quite a sight. Huck it was all meaningless without you. I mean I looked out on that congest and I couldn't see anybody like I was blind and the world had whited out. Like that quick second after the flashbulb done burst.

I ain't going on again. Mama says you're coming back when you're rich and ready. I'm horny without you.

I'm flesh-lonely.

Write again real quick I need your letters to feel you here.

Real love and all.

Hominy

Dear Honey-Hominy,

Sorry I hadn't written sooner. I been so busy here the box factory is going great guns and they're talking about putting on some extra folk and making some promotions.

I found a little club near work where the music isn't so bad and they let negroes cut up a little without calling the law so quick. I've been spending some nights there, me and Alligator and some others.

I'll send some money back soon as I can. I ran into a little trouble with the rent but I'll get that straightened and be on easy street soon. Bet on it. Laurie says I'm on my way.

I'll write back soon as I get some more time.

love,

Huck

Dear Huck-honey,

Your letter found me longing for you and hungry for news and I read that sucker must have been twenty times. (It was easy you didn't have much to say I guess) (Just teasing, but write more, do.) The Club is still working me till my back aches but Mr. Burro says the sales are down some. I don't know, seems like we been busy enough most nights. Sometimes though there's just me and Cal and Burt the Bartender (I forget you don't know Burt he took your place, well he took the place of the guy who took your place—Cal says he's hung like a painting but you probably don't want to hear that—after you split though he's no Huck Mr. Burro's fond of saying) and the place seems like an empty galaxy.

Oh Huck, Bessie Smith came through last week, a few days after Cotton Makers I guess it was. Came right into our club, sat down front, listened to the music for a while (it was Old Mama Redbone and I do believe she was so nervous at having the lady herself down front she kept forgetting the words and making up her own and some of the things she came out with were a downright hoot I tell you) and when she got up to leave, with her man on her arm, the whole place stood and clapped, you never seen anything like it. It was royalty was what it was.

I wished you could have been there.

Aw Huck. I want to see you. I will learn to live with the fact that I can't. I am lost in you and I guess I've got to find my way out.

Please write me soon as I live for your letters.

your honeydo,

Hominy

Dear Honey,

Don't worry about the club. It'll work out. That club's a Beale club and it'll be there when the rapture comes. Count on it.

My job here is still ok. Things are a little slow.

I got a new address I'll have to give it to you. The old place wasn't working out so good.

This new club I been going to is interesting. The other night the band played "Wiggling Harper Blues" and I thought of you. That's the song you used to carry on so much about, isn't it. It was something like that.

I hadn't seen Alligator in some time. I think he moved up east.

I'm working on some things. I'll be back in touch real quick. Don't carry on so, sugar.

Huck

Dear Huck,

I cannot function when I am at the mercy of despair—truly I cannot eat, or work, or talk. I lose the desire to go on.

You will tire of my discouragement I know. I don't really know what to say. I'm anxious, angst-ridden, angry even. I have a lot of things to figure out. Maybe I should be a fatalist like Mama.

The club seems so dead these days, the whole of Beale. I swear sometimes it's a ghost town here. There are rumblings among the club owners about declining business; some talk of moving on, up east, and elsewhere. Last week we had a few days where no one came in, No One. The new bartender was out sick and it didn't matter and it made the club seem like an empty cell.

The Club was my world, was where I lived. Without the Club am I dead? Oh and you were my world, Huck and the club, used to be one thing. Used to be The Thing. Hominy's reason for being.

I go home nights and my house doesn't recognize me. My things all piled up and useless, someone else's things. I walk around like a survivor after a war, pick up a phonograph record or a spoon and look at it and it all seems so strange. No one calls, no one comes by.

Callie has left the club and is stripping in New Orleans, I believe she said. I ain't heard from her.

Sorry to sound so down, honey. Please please write soon.

love and delicious tongue kisses,

Hominy

Dear Hominy,

Sorry to be so long writing. Been on the move.

I need to talk to you, explain some things. About me and Laurie. About me.

Don't worry.

Huck

Dear Huck,

What's going on? It's so long between letters and then this half-finished card. What about you and Laurie? What about us? Oh, Huck. Come back to Beale. Come back soon.

If Beale is still here, I mean, I think the street's dying, baby. Days go by and I see no one. Mr. Burro has shut down the club, he says temporarily. Temporarily means no money.

I need you, Huck honey. Please let me know soon when you can come back, things aren't good here. I want to hold you. I need your hands and your breath on my neck . . . you take it from there. Please.

I feel like if you came back everything would be all right. This is fantasy I know. But it's all so empty without you, maybe if you were here, the club would come alive again, you were always so popular. Huck, I'm losing everything.

Write and tell me when you can come see me. We need to get together, we can make it good again, I swear.

I love you.

your Honey

Dear Huck,

It's been three weeks. I can't do this alone. I can't keep this up from my end alone.

Where are you? With you gone the world is abandoned for me. Please just write and tell me you're ok.

Beale Street is dead. All the bars are closed. I can't even find Mr. Burro to ask about BingoBango. I'm hungry.

It's so lonely here. I haven't seen another living soul for days, maybe longer. I'm losing weight. The world's losing weight.

I need to hear from you.

Hominy

Dear Huck,

I swear if I could get to Cincinnati I would come there and recover you. I realize now you ain't gonna write me back.

Your life goes on without me.

Are you ok? Do you ever get lonely?

Huck, remember the good times.

Please, come find me.

Hominy

Dear Huck,

The leaves are falling off all the trees on our street. That ginkgo we loved is dying, I think, something other than seasonal departure at work down in its roots. I love Memphis because of all the trees and autumn always makes me a little sad, as if all my friends were changing or moving on without me. It's just a cycle Mama used to say, God's plan for constant renewal.

If it wasn't for the trees and the cooler winds I wouldn't know where we are in the year. My calendar still says June and I haven't had the initiative to change it and now I've lost track and wouldn't know where to pick up again.

I found a new handbill in the street today, one I haven't seen before, advertising some new act I hadn't heard of, playing at some club I hadn't heard of. At first I thought it was a sign of new life, someone with a little hope moving here with a plan to set things up and get something going again. But it had blown here from somewhere else, somewhere beyond the river maybe, maybe from Cincinnati. Maybe it's from the club where you go, maybe it's someone you know.

Nothing else is new on the street these days. All the buildings look gray and useless and the paint's flaking on the signs and the posters all are for shows and folks long gone. Sometimes I walk outside from one end of Beale to the other and maybe I see Old Riverbones, maybe I see nobody. A few days ago, how many I don't know, Old Riverbones stopped me and asked me my name. It's only cause he's getting old I guess, I guess he knows me about as well as anybody. We talked a few minutes about the old days and he seemed a little confused—time is all skimble-scambled in his head—it's what happens to the mind, to the world—and allowed as to how he was probably moving on himself, up river he said, and I would've laughed except it struck me as kind of sad.

Mama died. They took her body up east to where her family is. I couldn't go.

This morning I went out to look around. I was getting the heebie-jee-bies sitting around that apartment with the walls getting blanker and more threatening and I had to rush out for a breath of air.

I walked down to Beale and wandered in and out of doorways, looked into grimy windows and shady doors. Stood for a while outside the pawn shop and tried to make out each item there, left abandoned and unwanted. I went over to BingoBango and stood in the entranceway and looked through the glass and the tables were all standing there ready as if the show was going on tonight. Remember, Huck, that night Mr. Handy was playing and you were tending bar and I was just a newcomer there all nervous and hoping for big tips. And that white woman was coming on to you and you were so cool back there—all the gals wanted you—and you had your eyes on me and we were sort of locked into each other and we knew it and little had to be said. That white woman just wandered away all sad-eyed and I came up to that bar later and you said Your name Honey and I didn't want to embarrass you and said Yes Yes my name's Honey and for a long time that's all you called me, for a goodly time after that.

I thought I heard somebody in the back of BingoBango and I tapped lightly on the glass but I knew it was just a rat or something. Nobody's been in there for months.

It was so quiet it was the end of the world.

I meandered down the street, moving pointlessly, and it struck me like a revelation. Everybody's gone. Everybody isn't here anymore, and I tried to remember when the last time I had seen another human being was and I couldn't do it. There are no more people.

And I stood there in the middle of Beale and I started crying and I let those tears fall all the way down, down onto the street. I cried a river, I let my tears flow down to Beale and I was crying for the losses, for the loss of the world, for the old lonely world. I wept for the heartache in all of us. I wept for the empty spaces, for the ends of things. I wept for the way things were and the way things won't be no more.

And I stood there alone on that spot and I figured I just had to go on home and a wind started blowing, a murmuring wind with musical under-tones. There's no one anywhere and the wind's blowing down Beale, and it sounded like old voices.

I love you.

Hominy

COREY MESLER has been published in numerous anthologies and journals including *Poetry, Gargoyle, Five Points, Good Poems, American Places,* and *New Stories from the South.* He has published nine novels, four short story collections, five full-length poetry collections, and a dozen chapbooks. His novel, *Memphis Movie,* attracted kind words from Ann Beattie, Peter Coyote, and William Hjortsberg, among others. He's been nominated for the Pushcart many times, and three of his poems were chosen for Garrison Keillor's *The Writer's Almanac.* He also wrote the screenplay for *We Go On,* which won the Memphis Film Prize in 2017. With his wife he runs a 143-year-old bookstore in Memphis. He can be found at https://coreymesler.wordpress.com.

6

The Planning Meeting for Bringing College Classes to the Local Prison Takes a Weird Turn

Kathleen Founds

After Count of Monte Cristo.

DEAN OF HUMANITIES I'm delighted to see this project finally moving forward. And I'm glad to see Nicole here today, representing adjunct English faculty. But I don't exactly feel comfortable sending adjuncts into a room of prisoners. Will Nicole be in there all by herself?

SHERIFF Look, we're a minimum security county jail. And only nonviolent offenders with proven track records of good behavior will be eligible to enroll in classes.

HEAD OF ENGLISH DEPARTMENT Our faculty will surely bring up a host of concerns. Families need to know their loved ones will be safe in the workplace. For instance, how is Nicole's husband going to feel about her going into a prison, armed only with a dull pencil and a thin stack of comma splice worksheets? I mean, could Nicole fashion these items into weapons in a survival scenario? Of course. But what kind of close combat martial arts training will we provide for Nicole and other faculty members? And where will the funding for said programs come from?

DEAN OF SCIENCES And I can't help but notice Nicole is pregnant. How would we handle a scenario where she went into labor in the prison classroom, with only convicts to rely upon for emotional and medical support?

DEAN OF ENGINEERING More to the point—what if those convicts were to take her newborn baby and raise it as one of their own, feeding it with the milk of rats, tattooing it with their signs, and training it to fight in their ways? What if they were to release this child, once grown, into the ventilation ducts, to escape the prison and terrorize the populace? What would be our ethical and legal responsibilities, as an institution, in that eventuality?

DEAN OF SOCIAL SCIENCES I hate to say it, but litigation wise? Fiscally speaking? That fetus is a liability.

SHERIFF The program isn't set to start until 2019. I'm sure Nicole will have already delivered her baby by then. Hopefully, in a hospital.

NICOLE I'm actually planning to use a birthing center.

DEAN OF HUMANITIES That's what my wife did. Such a great experience.

DEAN OF SOCIAL SCIENCES Have we considered a scenario where Nicole's attempts to rehabilitate prisoners via liberal arts backfires, and instead, the prisoners convert *her* to the criminological mindset? During each class, when they are supposed to be composing well-constructed topic sentences, prisoners are downloading their criminal experience to Nicole, who in one short semester becomes a criminal mastermind. Now we have a scenario where Nicole has a criminological mind-set and access to the alarm codes for the copy room. Is this a risk we are willing to take?

DEAN OF HEALTH AND HUMAN SERVICES Have we considered a scenario where Nicole falls in love with one of the prisoners, who happens to be black, and embarks upon an illicit affair with him through subtle use of her podium as a screening device? Then, when her baby is born, it's *twins*, and one is white and one is *black*. How would her husband feel about *that*?

SHERIFF Look, Nicole is already pregnant. No matter how much illicit sex she has with the prisoners, she's not going to be impregnated with a black baby. I mean, unless her husband is black, and her baby is already black. Nicole, is your husband black?

NICOLE Uh . . . he's Latino.

DEAN OF HEALTH AND HUMAN SERVICES Well, there you go.

DEAN OF SOCIAL SCIENCES A half-black baby can pass as Latino. It's possible Nicole's husband wouldn't suspect anything. We may be blowing this whole situation out of proportion.

HEAD OF ENGLISH DEPARTMENT We could just have male faculty teach in the prison.

DEAN OF ENGINEERING Cuts down on rape risk.

DEAN OF SCIENCES But men can get raped, too.

PRESIDENT OF COLLEGE I mean, from a sociological perspective— and that's my academic background, before I moved into adminis- tration, and I still keep up with the periodicals—the social shame and stigma is worse for male rape victims. If Nicole were gang raped by a horde of sweaty, muscled, tattooed prisoners, everyone would feel sorry for her. But if a male faculty member was raped, students would question his masculinity.

DEAN OF ENGINEERING Actually? If Nicole was raped by the prison- ers, I believe the question on the community's mind would be, what was she wearing?

DEAN OF HUMANITIES Was it a skirt?

DEAN OF SCIENCES How short was it?

COLLEGE PRESIDENT If it goes up to here, that's just asking for it.

DEAN OF HUMANITIES Excuse me! This is *absolutely unacceptable*. It is *unconscionable* to get caught up in this inane minutia.

PRESIDENT OF COLLEGE I don't follow.

DEAN OF HUMANITIES There is one possibility that, in your preten-
tion and myopia, you have failed to even *consider*.

COLLEGE PRESIDENT By all means—enlighten us.

DEAN OF HUMANITIES Okay, so there could be this one prisoner—
let's call him Bruiser—whose prose is so electric, so alive, so
mind-blowingly brilliant that Nicole becomes consumed by envy.
Unable to bear the reality that Bruiser is a better writer, Nicole col-
ludes with another inmate to frame Bruiser for stabbing a prison
guard with a very sharp toothbrush. Unjustly condemned, Bruiser
marinates in wrath. He vows to revenge himself upon our college.
Bruiser spends the next twenty years scraping at the wall of his cell
with a plastic spoon. His patient toil is complemented by the equally
diligent digging of the mad priest in a neighboring cell. Soon, their
escape tunnels connect. They exchange their tragic tales and, via
joint tunneling effort, burrow to the edge of the prison grounds.
Alas, at the last moment, a cave-in occurs. The tunnel collapses on
the mad priest, crushing him. Before dying, he gives Bruiser a really
good stock tip. Bruiser trades places with his friend's corpse, hiding
beneath the burial shroud. After being wheeled out on a gurney,
Bruiser rises up from the autopsy table, overpowers the coroner, and
escapes through a window. Bruiser then uses the priest's excellent
stock tip to make some strategic short sales. After becoming a mil-
lionaire, Bruiser takes on the identity of a mysterious philanthro-
pist looking to endow our college. Seducing department heads with
the prospect of a million-dollar donation, Bruiser manipulates us
all until we turn against one another and the faculty senate erupts
with strife. At the same time, Bruiser tracks down Nicole's baby,
who is now a young man. Bruiser takes this young man under his
wing and introduces him to a life of crime and decadence. All is
ruined. Wrecked. Ravaged. We rend our garments and smear ashes
in our hair.

DEAN OF ENGINEERING ...

COLLEGE PRESIDENT But the faculty senate is *already* consumed with
strife.

HEAD OF ENGLISH DEPARTMENT Really. It can't get much worse.

DEAN OF HUMANITIES Ah. Excellent point. Touché.

SHERIFF Circling back to the rape issue—could we create wardrobe restrictions for female faculty? Prison-appropriate garb?

DEAN OF ENGINEERING Nicole, could you stand up for a moment? And just turn around a few times? What she's wearing now would be okay.

HEAD OF ENGLISH DEPARTMENT The pants are a little tight.

DEAN OF HEALTH AND HUMAN SERVICES You can really see the outline of Nicole's butt in those pants. Could be very suggestive to the prisoners.

NICOLE You know what? This whole meeting is weirding me out. I feel very uncomfortable.

COLLEGE PRESIDENT Okay. Male faculty it is.

KATHLEEN FOUNDS has worked at a nursing home, a phone bank, a South Texas middle school, and a midwestern technical college specializing in truck-driving certificates. She got her undergraduate degree at Stanford and her MFA at Syracuse. She teaches social justice–themed English classes at Cabrillo College in Watsonville, California, and writes while her toddler is napping. Her work has been published in the *Sun*, *Good Housekeeping*, the *New Yorker Online*, *McSweeney's Internet Tendency*, *Salon*, and *Booth*. Her novel-in-stories, *When Mystical Creatures Attack!*, won the 2014 University of Iowa Press John Simmons Short Fiction Award and was named a *New York Times* Notable Book.

7

LISTEN TO ME

Bryan Furuness

After The Odyssey.

SINON WAS A LITTLE GUY AND PRETTY USELESS WHEN IT CAME TO war. He wasn't strong like Eurymaches or superfast like Ajax the Lesser. He was a balding runt with a trick knee whose only real skill was bull-shitting—which is why Odysseus recruited him for the attack on Troy.

"Nights on a foreign shore can get tedious," said Odysseus. "We could use some talent around the campfire."

"Would I have to fight?" asked Sinon.

"Not if you don't want to."

Sinon looked around his extended-stay hovel. The sink had four coffee mugs in it, which marked the day as Wednesday. On one hand, the offer sounded like a solid, long-running gig. On the other hand, Odysseus had a reputation for being slippery. Was there a catch? "I'm a lover, not a fighter," he said, joking but not joking. "Just so we're clear on that point."

Odysseus gave him a broad smile. "If you were really a lover, you'd know that's the biggest fight of all."

"Seriously, though. Not a soldier. *Capisce*?"

Still smiling, Odysseus shook his hand. "Not a soldier."

The siege turned out to be a long, hard slog. The Greeks had superior weaponry and snazzy uniforms—the kind with boar tusks sewn into the leather, which didn't actually offer any extra protection, but, as big Eurymaches put it, "It's easier to fight when you look bitchin'." None of this helped against the Trojan wall.

The wall was built from boulders too huge to have been lifted by human hands. Where Sinon saw evidence of clever engineering, Odysseus suspected they'd gotten help from the gods. Odysseus saw the world through god-tinted lenses, which could be funny (like when he'd called a short-beaked dolphin following their ship an "emissary of Poseidon") but was more often terrifying (like when someone noticed that Ocytus missed dinner, and Odysseus remarked darkly, "Poseidon demanded a sacrifice").

The Trojans called the wall "The Equalizer," as in *Hey, I like how you're tapping that battering ram against The Equalizer. Adorable!* Or: *Look how your spears bounce right off. Pling, plong, pling. Score one for The Equalizer!*

The Trojans were a nation of hecklers. Not bold enough to attempt a single advance, they were content to hang out on top of the wall and make fun of those who did. As the Greeks flung themselves against the boulders, the Trojans counterattacked with cat-calls, jibes, Bronx cheers.

The Greeks built a catapult, but the wall was too high and their fireballs exploded showily against the stones (*Rejected by The Equalizer!*). Arrows and spears disappeared harmlessly over the parapets until Odysseus told his guys to quit wasting ammunition. They uprooted entire trees to bash against the gate, which led the Trojan guards to speculate loudly about the Greeks' sexual ineptitude. Whenever the soldiers attempted to scale the wall, the guards poured down a mixture of used cooking oil and raw sewage. They could have boiled the oil, or sent down a hail of spears, but what fun would that have been? It was funnier to see your enemies fall to the ground and then try to help each other up with slickery, crap-covered hands.

Every night the Greeks trudged back to their camp on the shore, exhausted and reeking, which made a tough crowd for Sinon. But every night he came up with fresh material—observational stuff mainly, riffing on that day's battle. "Someone should teach Ajax the Lesser how to throw a spear. Seriously, 'Jax, you look like you're trying to fling snot off your hand."

Another storyteller might have caught a knife in the ribs for that crack, but Less just smirked while the other guys jostled him good-naturedly. These guys loved Sinon. His nightly performance was the best part of their day. And Sinon grew to love them back. These were *his* guys. He'd never had guys before. Or anyone, really. Since his mother had died, his whole life had been a solo act. Which had been fine. Or, not fine, but not terrible. A gray life. Nothing like this. On the beach, he did an impression of Lesser throwing a spear, complete with a pratfall on the follow-through, and when his face hit the sand, he heard the roar of laughter that never got old, followed by shouts of *Do another! Do me! Do Eurymaches trying to count past ten!*

After a year, the war settled into a lower gear. Most of the soldiers gave up and went home to their wives and farms and Senate duties. The ones who stuck around were the single guys who had nothing better to do, and who were, frankly, really enjoying this war. The daily battles had become perfunctory. The Greeks still went to the wall every morning, but skirmishes were reduced to schoolyard taunting, the Trojans trying to trick them into range of the sewage pots, Odysseus yelling at his guys to "take the battle serious."

At lunch, guards and soldiers would share techniques for roasting goats, rib each other about their respective tastes in cheese, and occasionally declare a truce to foot-race along the shoreline. The Greeks cleared some land for planting, and the Trojans gave them tips on farming the sandy soil. In exchange, the Greeks taught them how to make columns out of sheared cypress trees, and, weeks later, the tops of a few clumsy columns were visible inside The Equalizer.

All in all, it was a good war. Casualties were low, morale was high. The only one who still talked about "winning" was Odysseus, who was also the only one anxious to get home. For Sinon, the situation was perfect. He was getting paid to bullshit around a campfire with his friends. The ocean hushed him to sleep. He ate fresh fish and took long walks along the shoreline and had to cut about a foot off his rope belt, he'd slimmed down so much. What more could he want? This was before he met Cassandra.

Several years into the siege, the poets and prophets of Troy proposed a "cultural exchange program." Sinon agreed to bring the idea to Odysseus, though he was sure it would get nixed on the spot. By this time, the siege was doing terrible things to the big man's mind and worse things to his mood. He spent his days alone in his tent, slugging down wine and periodically yelling at the gods as though they were nagging him. *Get off my ass!* he could be heard to shout at least once an hour. *I know, I know* was another common one, though what he knew, exactly, no one knew.

But Sinon had promised to ask, so he went to Odysseus's tent and he asked. Then he waited for his rebuke, trying not to breathe the goaty air as Odysseus, spread-eagle on the ground, stared up at the drooping canopy. His eyes were doing a crazy waterbug dance. "Tell you what," said Sinon after a solid minute of silence. "I'll put them off, tell them maybe next year."

"Now."

Sinon was already halfway out the tent flap. He took a sip of fresh air before coming back in. "What?"

"Now is good," said Odysseus to the canopy. His voice was syrupy with wine. "We are ready for this."

"Ready for this," Sinon repeated carefully. "Are we still talking about the exchange program?"

"Exchange program," echoed Odysseus, as though relaying a message to the ceiling. "Yes."

Sinon shifted his weight. Was Odysseus being slippery, or just shit-faced? "I've got to know," said Sinon. "Is this some kind of trick?"

A smile spread across the big man's face, though his eyes were still spaced-out. "That's what I should have asked before getting into this mess," Odysseus said. "You're so smart, Sinon. You should be me."

Sinon forced a chuckle. "Me? I'm no leader."

"*Leader.*" Odysseus shook his head, and when it came to rest he was looking at Sinon's foot. When he spoke again, his voice was even softer. "The guys, they think this is all my doing, but it's not . . . they push me around, Sinon."

"They?"

Flies tapped against the canvas, searching for a way out. Odysseus blinked, unseeing. His breath was terrible, a carcass in the sun. "I'm a plaything of the gods," he breathed. "A character in someone else's story."

His eyes were scuffed with cataracts, full of clouds and pleading. Sinon had never seen such a helpless look in his life. What did Odysseus want from him? Help, friendship, a different story to star in?

Before he could ask, the big man closed his eyes. Sinon checked his pulse—still alive, *whew*—then hustled to the gate to pass on the good news about the cultural exchange.

After their campfire gigs were over, the culturati from both sides got together outside the main gate to drink and gossip and steal each other's stories. Troy was a small town, *très* provincial, the insiders complained, and they were starving for material. "Not that you would understand," they told Sinon. "Greece is so metropolitan. Plus, you guys attack people. That's *active*. Try working with a wall as your protagonist."

For the first month of the exchange, Sinon stiffened every time a twig snapped, sure that Odysseus was about to storm out of the bushes to lay waste to poets, but eventually his suspicions of trickery died down. By then the exchange had devolved into bitch sessions, but Sinon kept going anyway because of Cassandra.

She was a prophetess, which would have been sexy enough to drive Sinon wild even if it hadn't been for her full lips, her heavy eyelids, everything about her suggesting a ripe fruit bending the end of a branch. She had this big, throaty laugh that gave Sinon a shivery feeling, like bubbles were fizzing up his ribcage.

He couldn't look at a roasted goat leg without wondering if Cassandra liked goat and what her thoughts were *vis-à-vis* cooking on a spit, which somehow led him to wonder what she tasted like. He spent more time working up material for the cultural exchange than for his own campfire. He wanted, more than anything, to make her laugh, and then laugh again, a sound he came to think of as his heart going *jackpot, jackpot*. Also, he wanted to murder any other man who made her laugh.

But why bother? She was light-years out of his league. He told himself to give up, but doom only magnified his romantic feelings. She caught him staring at least three times a night, and each time he had to pretend he was spacing out or that there was something interesting just over her shoulder.

Looking at Cassandra was like drinking saltwater: it made you thirstier and thirstier, and then you went insane. Sinon tried skipping the cultural exchange, but it turned out that not being around her made him feel even worse.

During the day, he still went for long walks along the shoreline, but slowly now, and when he got far away from camp, he'd scream into his hands or punch the wet sand until it felt like his wrists were splintering. Somehow this was more satisfying than masturbating, which he also did on these walks. All it took was one thought of Cassandra unwrapping her gauzy clothing, revealing, little by little, her navel, which would be oblong like a tiny boat—and then Sinon lit into the brush for some privacy, hoping that none of the scrub was poisonous and knowing he wouldn't be able to stop himself if it was.

Eight years into the siege, Odysseus declared that he wanted to build a wooden horse. Before they could start the project, they had to buy tools from the Trojans, who (of course) scalped them on the deal. Then they had to dismantle one of their ships to get the building materials. Even then, construction was slow going, because these Greeks were warriors, not carpenters.

They built it in front of the main gate, because that was part of the deal with the Trojans: If at any point it started to look like a megaweapon, the Trojans could crush it with heavy boulders they had balanced on top of the parapets.

"What is that thing?" one of the Trojan poets asked Sinon one night. At that point, it was just a wooden box frame with big wheels.

"Big surprise," said Sinon, who was frankly a little embarrassed for Odysseus. It was one thing for the Greeks to make fun of him, but he didn't want the Trojan snarksters knowing that the big man was out of his damn mind. "You're gonna love it."

"This is bad," said Cassandra. "Really bad."

One poet rolled his eyes to Sinon. "She's always saying shit like that. If we made a drinking game out of her warnings, we'd all have cirrhosis."

"Women be warning, women be *warning*," said a drunken harpist.

Cassandra shook her head at the fire. "All you jerks are going to die."

"Yeah. Someday."

She stamped her foot. "Assholes! You are looking at the machine of your execution."

A sculptor leaned over to the poet. "That's the real reason you can't make a drinking game out of her warnings," he said. "She'll kill your buzz every time."

Sniggering, they exchanged a sloppy high five. Cassandra stared at them, then grabbed the cold end of a flaming log. Before anyone could stop her, she flung it onto the wooden chassis. For a shocked second, no one moved—and then the poets were kicking sand over the log and yelling that she was as bad as Odysseus with his hard-on for war. "Fucking relax!" the sculptor shouted at her before drawing back to the campfire.

Cassandra stayed by the chassis, frowning at the charred spot. Sinon stayed with her. In the air was a tang of tar and salt and singed cedar. "They never listen," she said.

"So why bother telling them anything?"

She lifted her chin toward Odysseus's tent down the beach, the only one blazing with light. "Why does he bother with the siege?"

"Maybe he hopes he'll wear you guys down."

"Maybe he can't help himself," she said. "Maybe he can't stop."

"He says the gods make him do it."

Sinon delivered this line like a straight man, hoping she would snort and they could sarcasm-bond over Odysseus's weird beliefs. But she only pulled her shawl around herself and started back to the campfire. Over her shoulder, she said, "Maybe they do."

The next night Sinon heard a weary note in Cassandra's laugh. Was that new, or was he just now noticing it? Maybe laughter was her shield, one that kept her from breaking down or lashing out at everyone who refused to listen. Either laughter kept her from looking crazy, or it kept her from going crazy.

But once in a while there came a moment, late at night, when she stopped laughing, when she let down her shield and showed herself to be tired and hurt and hopeful, and for this reason, Sinon began staying at the campfire longer than anyone else. These moments were rare and short, and he didn't want to miss a single one.

One night she asked him to tell her about Greece.

It was late. The fire had died down to winking embers, and the sky was rimmed with red, the dawn of dawn. The only sound was the sea. All the other bards and prophets and lutists and playwrights had either wobbled back inside the gate or passed out by the horse.

Sinon looked at her closely. Was she screwing with him? There wasn't enough light to see if she was smirking or mock-batting her eyes. If he answered sincerely, she might bray out a laugh and shove him off the log. He'd seen her punk more than one poet in this way—drawing him out of his shell of irony and lazy cynicism, exposing the tender mollusk of his heart, and then, *bam. Gotcha, dumbass.* Sinon had always laughed with her, thinking of her as a poseur exposer, but what if he was her next victim? His mollusk couldn't take it.

On the other hand, how many of these moments would he get?

Sinon took a chance. He told her about his Greece, how he remembered it. With his fingers, he drew a picture on the slate sky, sketching out the wide avenues, the hammered bronze sundials, the harbor that glittered like the eye of Zeus. Every time she said *Hmm* or laughed softly, his soul got the bends.

And then he was describing *her* walking down that wide avenue, dust from a passing chariot settling in her hair. Cassandra, buying plums in the marketplace and bringing them to his, Sinon's, home. And then—he could hardly believe he was saying this—she came into his home, set down the plums, took Sinon in her arms, ran her fingers into the little curls on the back of his head, and kissed him full on the lips.

In the first ray of dawn, Cassandra looked at him with a serious expression. His stomach turned into a plum pit.

"This is never going to work," she murmured as she leaned toward him. Sometimes, apparently, she didn't listen to herself, either. When she curled her fingers into his hair, Sinon went blind with ecstasy.

This became their time: the hour before dawn. For a while, it was enough. For a while, the time seemed longer than it really was, because Sinon spent each morning replaying mental highlights from the night before, and in the evenings he visualized how their time would go that night. Sometimes they made out with an intensity that gave Sinon toe cramps; sometimes they just talked. Well, Sinon talked. He told her everything about himself, holding nothing back. He was amazed at what came out of his mouth. Stuff that was awful, shameful! Stuff you don't tell girls, ever, because they will be repulsed! Like: After his mother died, he wrote letters to her. "That's kind of sweet," said Cassandra. "That's not the end of the story," said Sinon. After a while he started mailing those letters to himself so he would have mail. And then—okay, this part made him cringe to remember it—he started writing the letters in his mother's voice. *My dearest boy, I hope you are well and not eating too much cheese*, and so on.

Like also: This fantasy he entertained a few months earlier, in which all the soldiers and guards killed each other in one fantastic blood-orgy so that the only two people left in the city were him and her. "Well, you can't spell bloodlust without lust," she allowed.

Or, finally: He was a virgin. He wasn't even sure what a vagina looked like, much less how it worked. "What do you think it looks like?" she asked, and when he drew his best guess in the sand with a stick, she laughed soundlessly and toppled over. Sinon had never seen anything sexier in his life. "All these years," she gasped, "you've been dreaming about fucking *a kraken's beak*. Boy, are you gonna be disappointed when you see mine."

He jizzed on his own thigh, spontaneously, like a hiccup. For the next three days that phrase played in his head on a constant loop—*When you see mine, when you see mine, when you see mine*—keeping him awake and crazy.

Cassandra told him about herself, too, though not as much or as freely. Now and again, she'd reveal a glimpse of her girlhood (tomboy, watercolors, fistfights) or life inside The Equalizer (cliquish, boring: "Honestly, the invasion is the best thing to happen to Troy in years. You guys are like a road show.") but if Sinon asked any follow-ups, she clammed up. He told himself to be patient. Receptive, not probing. After years of talking to people who failed to listen, Cassandra would need some time to trust him, to love him like he loved her.

Yes: love. How else to explain the constant clutch in his throat, the urge to declaim poetry? Sometimes during the day he walked into the brush and wept with gratitude until he passed out from exhaustion. Once he got up completely covered with ants. As he started back to camp, it felt like a message from the gods. As he got closer to the tents, it felt more like a wondrous joke. Stumbling with giddiness and eager to show his friends (*Aargh! I'm Ant-man!*), he inhaled a bunch of ants and fell to his knees, hacking, ants rolling off him like water.

Days flew past. The siege dragged on. The horse took shape: the spine, the blocky head. Sinon and Cassandra kept their relationship secret, being careful not to act too friendly (or to feign too much distance) while anyone else was awake around the campfire. Acting normal turned out to be the hardest role. But once the others drifted away and the turret guards slumped over, they had their hour. It was still good, but Sinon wanted more.

"Come to my tent," he said.

"Sinon . . ."

"No one has to know," he said, threading his fingers through hers. "If you want, I can make love so that even you won't know."

"That I believe," she said, but she still wouldn't budge from the campfire.

One night he snaked a hand into the sleeve of her toga, but she trapped it between her elbow and ribcage, clamping down hard enough to pop a knuckle. "Be happy with what you have," she said through her teeth. If anyone found out about them, they'd call it collusion or treason. And if Odysseus found out? Shit, meet fan.

"Or," Sinon suggested, "maybe it would end the war. Think about it: our, uh, marriage could usher in a new era of peace between our nations."

She shook her head in disbelief. "Just like all the others, aren't you? Can't listen to a damn thing I say."

That night, Sinon understood something about Odysseus. Of all the men on the beach, only the two of them knew what it was like to stand so close, for so long, to something you desperately wanted and not to get it. Only the two of them knew the particular madness of Tantalus.

A few months earlier, the siege had been a kind of limbo, and that had seemed like paradise to Sinon. Now that limbo felt like hell.

Sinon needed a plan. He just didn't imagine that someone else would come up with one for him.

Sinon was asleep under the horse when Eurymaches came for him. He was supposed to be checking for loose pegs but had drifted off.

Big E stuck a toe in his ribs. "Odysseus wants to see you." He bent down and took a sharp sniff. "Go dip in the ocean first, man. You stink like campfire. And perfume."

Sinon's gut clenched. "Oh, *that*," he said in what he hoped was a super-casual tone. "Yeah, I was weeding the flower garden. Perfume, ha."

"Weeding?" Eurymaches scratched his beard thoughtfully. "Was that before or after you were necking with that prophetess?"

Sinon's whole body went cold. Eurymaches laughed and slugged his thigh. "Dude, everyone *knows*," he said. None of the guys cared, he assured Sinon, though they were all surprised a hairy gnome like him could land a hot soothsayer. "Is it true what they say about prophetesses?" Eurymaches asked him. "That their vaginas are like a kraken's—"

"Does Odysseus know?"

His heart was floating up. If Odysseus knew, that must mean he was cool with it, in which case Sinon could run to Cassandra right now and—

"No," said Eurymaches, all the teasing gone out of his face. "He hasn't stuck his head outside his tent for weeks. And if you're smart, you'll realize that his ignorance is your bliss." Eurymaches cuffed him on the side of the head. "Seriously, go wash up. The big man might be a little distracted, but he's got a nose."

Sinon watched him go, thinking, *What a decent guy*. Then he got up and tripped over his laces that Eurymaches had tied together before waking him.

The front of Odysseus's tent faced Troy; the rear faced Greece. When Sinon came up, wet from the sea, he saw Odysseus standing at the open back of the tent, gazing across the water, directly into the setting sun. Sinon wondered if Odysseus was a little blind, stone crazy, or both. At least he was upright this time.

"We cannot win out here," said Odysseus in a flat voice without looking at Sinon. "We have to get inside those walls."

Sinon grunted. *You and me both, pal.*

The sun touched the sea, setting the horizon on fire. "The horse is hollow," said Odysseus. "We're going to fill it with warriors then set them loose once it's inside the wall."

Sinon's mouth fell open. The Trojans would never see that coming. After heckling the construction effort for years, any suspicions they'd had were long forgotten. They considered the horse a folly, another Greek vanity, a hobby to distract the warriors from the futility of their siege.

Still, the plan was missing a step.

"How are you going to get the horse inside the wall?" said Sinon.

As the sun bled out in the ocean, Odysseus regarded Sinon with his scuffed eyes. "That," he said, "is where you come in."

The next morning, Odysseus approached the main gate with a scowl and a fresh tunic, acting more like his old hale self than he had in years. "Congratulations, assholes!" he shouted to the guards and noblemen who had gathered atop the wall to watch the Greeks burn their tents and board their ships. "You did what the mighty Poseidon could not do with his cruel dolphins, what Zeus could not do with his—"

"What's the trick?" called one of the guards.

"No trick," yelled Odysseus. "We're just done here. Ten years is enough. Nice job repulsing us. Be proud. You'll tell your grandchildren about this day."

He spat in the sand, tromped across the beach, boarded the final ship, and, to the Trojans' amazement, cast off.

But after the ship disappeared around the coast, just as they were all enjoying a chant of *EEE-qua-LI-zer (clap-clap, clap-clap-clap)*, a lone figure came trudging back up the beach. The crowd went silent, straining to see who it was and what it could mean. As usual, Cassandra was the first to twig. On the parapet, she clucked her tongue. "Sinon."

When Sinon declared that he loved Cassandra more than his home country and that he wished to defect, it touched off a big debate. As usual, the argument broke along class lines. The guards were sure he wanted to infiltrate their defenses, and they proposed to kill him on the spot, "just to be safe." The noblemen, who had supported the cultural exchange from the beginning, thought it was the most romantic gesture they'd ever seen, and who were they to stand in the way of love? Besides, even if the guards were right, who cared? The war was *over*, meatheads. How much damage could one balding runt do?

They argued back and forth, and one of the guards took a pot shot at Sinon with a clumsily thrown spear, and eventually King Priam was summoned to the wall.

Sinon stood back as the main gate opened, and Priam tottered forth with a retinue of guards who didn't look so cocksure out in the open. The old man stopped and licked his lips, which Sinon took as an invitation to explain himself. "Your highness," he said in a voice loud enough to be heard by the crowd. "My body may be outside your walls, but my heart lives in your city. My prayer is that, in your mercy, you will take me in. But if not"—Sinon's voice rose stagily like he'd planned, but he was surprised to find that the emotion behind it felt real—"I ask that you kill me now, because life apart from my beloved is not life at all."

A nobleman sighed huskily. One of the guards muttered, "My ass."

Priam licked his lips again. Sinon leaned in to listen.

"Nice horse," Priam said. "Your guys just left it behind?"

Cassandra stepped through the gate. "Dad. . ."

Sinon's eyes widened. Looking at Cassandra, he mouthed, *Dad?*

Priam said, "It would look nice in the plaza." He half turned to Cassandra. "Wouldn't it look nice in the plaza?"

She shook her head slowly. "This is not a good idea."

"No?" Priam sounded surprised. "Where would you put it?"

This fired up an argument they'd clearly had before. Cassandra said he never listened to her, and Priam wondered why she didn't want him to be happy. As they flung examples at one another, the underlying pattern became clear: Cassandra warned, Priam said *Bah* and got his way, and though he was always sorry later, the pattern kept repeating itself.

Priam was going to get his way again, Sinon realized with a feeling like ants pouring off his body. Odysseus's plan was going to work. Sinon had not anticipated this. In fact, the only reason he'd agreed to play his part was because he thought there was no way the stupid plan would work. Or, rather, he thought only the *first* part would work—the part where he defected.

But the second part? Where Odysseus told him to claim that the horse was a giant talisman that would protect the owner from any future invasions? Sinon wasn't even going to try that part. His own plan was to get his ass inside the wall and leave the horse behind. The gates would close, and eventually his friends would bust out of the horse. Then they could all go back to the stalemate they'd enjoyed for the last decade, only Sinon would be inside with Cassandra.

"I'll take it," said Priam.

Inside the horse, something rustled. Sinon yelped a nervous laugh.

Priam cocked his head. "Son, what's the problem?"

Besides the fact that you're inviting destruction into your city? Sinon didn't say this, of course. If the Trojans caught on that the horse was rigged, they'd probably feel betrayed that the Greeks were suddenly taking the war seriously and retaliate by lighting the horse on fire, in which case his friends would be roasted like goats. Sinon was going to need his finest bullshit to get them all out of this mess.

He waited for the right words to rise into his mind.

Any minute now.

"Here's the deal," Priam said, taking Sinon by the shoulder. "I get the horse; you get citizenship." Ducking his head, he spoke out of the side of his mouth. "I make no promises about my daughter."

Cassandra looked toward the ocean. "You don't want to do this," she said, her earrings chiming her disapproval.

Priam didn't listen to her, of course. And it wasn't until later that Sinon realized she had been talking to both of them.

"Deal," said Sinon, because what else could he say? His voice was husky with emotion, which caused the noblemen to clutch at their hearts.

↓

Priam's deal made more sense once Sinon walked into the city. The columns he'd seen from the beach were the tip of the imitation iceberg. The guards in the king's retinue had tried to Greekify their helmets by sewing on pieces of boar tusk, though the tusky chunks flapped around like hangnails. Windowsill pottery appeared to have been rubbed with ash to give it that distinctive Greek coloration. In the chariot, Priam kept throwing his arm around Sinon as if to say, *Look at my Greek friend!*

Could Odysseus have known how much their siege had warped the Trojans? Sinon dismissed the thought. This was a dash of luck, that was all, and it could still be undone. Even now, Cassandra was trying to talk Priam out of his decision, though she didn't seem to be trying real hard. "You should really think this through," she said halfheartedly from the back of the chariot, apparently laying the groundwork for one hell of an *I told you so.*

Priam ignored her. "Check out the frescoes," he told Sinon. On a dirty wall was a crude illustration of a hugely endowed Priam strangling Odysseus. That's what the caption said, anyway. To Sinon's eyes, it looked like a watercolor painted by blind children in the rain.

"Admit it," Sinon forced himself to say. "You kidnapped a Greek artist to paint that, didn't you?" Priam shook his head shyly. Sinon took in all the rickety columns and tombstone pottery. "It's like I've died and gone to Athens!"

"Zeus," muttered Cassandra. Sinon's stomach was filled with plum pits.

Their chariot pulled into the plaza at the center of the city, followed by the horse, rumbling over the rutted streets, only some of the groans coming from the wooden joints. "Fucker's heavy!" complained one of the guards pushing the chassis, and the guy next to him nodded sagely. "Quality workmanship."

That night was a hot time in Old Troy. Not only had they repulsed Odysseus—he'd admitted it himself! How awesome was that!—they'd snagged an all-time piece of war booty. "Usually you have to go overseas to do your pillaging," Priam drolled to the noblemen who lined up to congratulate him. "How considerate of Odysseus to save us a trip."

The night was warm with a steady salt breeze. The plaza was alive with soldiers and poets and children, everyone drinking wine and making up songs about what pussies the Greeks were. At least twice an hour someone climbed up on the horse and made wild rodeo gestures, thinking he was the first one to come up with such a bold and hilarious idea.

On a balcony overlooking the plaza, Sinon and Cassandra silently shared a jug of wine. He cleared his throat several times before asking her, "How come you didn't tell me your father was the king?"

She gave him a dark look. "You are not in a position to lecture me about secrets." Then she lobbed the jug at the horse. It exploded against the neck, leaving a dark trail like a wound. A few Trojans backed away, shaking glass out of their hair. *Crazy bitch*, someone muttered.

"Let's run away." Sinon grabbed her hand. "Right now. We'll find a small island and make a home under an olive tree."

She made her hand small and slid it away. "I'm supposed to run away with the guy who's about to slaughter my people?"

He rubbed his forehead fiercely. There had to be a way out of this. There was *always* a way. Odysseus had known this, which is why he'd waded through a decade of futility and frustration. The difference here was that Sinon only had a few hours.

"I could just . . . not let them out of the horse," said Sinon. "They can't slaughter anyone from the inside."

"They'd starve or be discovered and burned alive. You'd let that happen to your friends?"

Sinon squeezed his eyes shut, dropped his head back. "How did this happen?" he said to the roof. "How on earth did this happen?"

Cassandra sighed. "Idiot," she said tenderly. "Odysseus knew about us. We were part of his plan." Her fingers curled into his hair. "We *were* his plan."

As dawn came near, the party faded. Revelers slipped back into houses, or into the palace, which Priam had opened for the night. The poets were the last to fall. Blind with wine, most of them passed out in the plaza.

Cassandra and Sinon were awake, of course. It was almost time for him to climb down from the balcony, arms and legs trembling. In the belly of the horse was a little door. Sinon would unlock it, then back away to watch the cramped soldiers drop out and crawl away like ants.

Cassandra would find her sleeping father and kiss him on the forehead without waking him—no use alerting him; he would just say *Bah*—before withdrawing to her room to await the invasion she already knew she would survive, though she wished she would not.

Sinon would return to Greece a hero, though he'd wish he were still a storyteller.

But all of that was still to come. Just then it was the hour before dawn, the hour that belonged to the two of them. Greek ships were already sailing back to Troy, ready to be let into the city, but for now Sinon was kneeling before Cassandra in a siege of tears, begging her to listen, to run with him, refusing to believe her as she tells him, over and over, that it is finished, they were characters in Odysseus's story, and now their part is over, all over.

BRYAN FURUNESS is the author of *The Lost Episodes of Revie Bryson*, a novel. With Michael Martone, he coedited the anthology *Winesburg, Indiana*. His stories can be found in *New Stories from the Midwest*, *Best American Nonrequired Reading*, and elsewhere. He lives in Indianapolis, where he teaches at Butler University.

8

DEAR NOBODY

Kirsty Logan

After Twenty Thousand Leagues Under the Sea.

07:00 / 01 March / lat 20 N long 40 W / temp -2°C
Strong currents from NE all day. Pressure good. Several shoals. Awake 16 hours.

Dear Nobody,

Last night I ventured out to hunt the squid. I swear I saw it. A glimpse of skull-sized eye, the twist and tentacle-grasp as it passed. A different squid than the one we fought, perhaps, but who can tell? Back then it was we, but now it's just me. I'm the only one left now. Me with my own deafening breath, tethered to the ship in my diving suit, floating with a gun in each hand in this depthless dark, cold to the marrow of my bones, the only hot blood for miles. I blink hard to see stars. Alone down here, I'm barely even a man anymore. But that was always the plan, wasn't it? ~~To lose our manhood, our humanity, in the hot blood of~~

23:44 / 03 March / lat 30 N long 40 W / temp -3°C
Currents calm. Out in suit to clear rudders, nothing to report. Awake 20 hours.

Dear Nobody,
Should we try again? We had such adventures. The coral reefs. The sunken wrecks. The ice shelves. We can follow the telegraph cable from coast to coast, slipping space-lost through the seas. We can rediscover Atlantis and lose it again. The sharks and the squid, our air-guns loaded with glass bullets.

Remember what we read about dead men? How over time coral builds up over the graves, sealing the bodies. How the dead sleep under the waves, out of the reach of sharks and men. ~~If we tried again, we could make so much coral~~

01:40 / 10 March / lat 35 N long 40 W / temp -1°C
Currents changeable. Whales. Seals. Awake 36 hours.

Dear Nobody,
I've been reading our books, eager to hear a voice in my head that isn't my own. Books always say that a thing is like another thing. The same might be said of us. Books always make me think of you, because you seem to be a lot of things while hiding what you really are. So here are the things that we are like:

The green-glow ruins of Atlantis, the carpet of bones, the silence. We found a volcano there, just like the one that ruined it all, but still alive, exploding underwater.

The undersea forest, the tall street of seaweeds that grew from the ocean floor, all the way to the surface. They grew straight and strong, and you said that when you bend one of the plants it immediately straightens itself again like nothing ever happened.

The—

Oh, this is useless.

It doesn't matter if you don't remember, Nemo. Just tell me we can try again. It could be different if you want, or it could be the same. ~~We got so good at those underwater funerals, we hid the men so holy, the coral will have grown, and the ocean is vaster than~~

23:44 / 30 April / lat 50 N long 60 W / temp -1°C
Some currents. Some pressure. Some sleep.

Dear Nobody,

When we first came to your ship, you let us believe you couldn't speak our language. You knew every word we said but let us speak because you wanted to know us, how we spoke when we thought you couldn't understand.

But now I think that you and I were the only ones who really spoke the same language. You said you were not a civilized man. You said you were finished with the world and would not obey its laws. Your words went right to the heart of me.

You taught me so much. The proper angles of smiles and frowns. The right times to agree and disagree. How to be friendly, how to feign sleep, how to prowl the submarine undetected. How to pass among them. How to be the last suspected.

I was shocked when I found out what you were doing, the person you truly were. I don't think I ever told you that. Perhaps shock is the wrong word: it was more a recognition. Like looking in the mirror when all you've seen before is windows. The clue is in the name, you said with a smile, standing there with the man still slumped and dripping in the corner and the blood thick up to your wrists. The name: Nemo. *No-man.* One need not be a man when exempt from the petty laws and morals of men. The things we did, the blood still to come on both our wrists. ~~So many sailors with no one to miss them when we~~

00:00 / May, perhaps / temp 0°C
No change.

Dear Nobody,

I said once that your words had touched my weak point, namely my great interest in learning. But that was never my weak point. You didn't even have to find it, because my weakness was yours. Was you.

You know I'm still here. You know, so why aren't you here? You know I'd never hurt you. ~~I only want us to be together again, so we can hurt~~

00:00 / 00 / 0°C

Dear Nobody,

I don't know where or when I am. It doesn't matter. All that matters is you. The blood, the last breaths, the souls we sent to rest. It means nothing without you.

If I surface, will you find me? Will they? I fear you have told them what we did. I traverse the endless ocean alone as a man on the run. A no-man. A wanted man, no longer wanted.

KIRSTY LOGAN is the author of the short story collection *The Rental Heart and Other Fairytales*, awarded the Polari First Book Prize and the Saboteur Award for Best Short Story Collection, and her debut novel *The Gracekeepers*, awarded a Lambda Literary Award. Her most recent book, *A Portable Shelter*, is a collection of linked short stories inspired by Scottish folktales and was published in a limited edition with custom woodblock illustrations. Her next novel, *The Gloaming*, is out in May 2018. She is currently working on a collection of short horror stories, a TV pilot script, and a musical collaboration project.

9

There Once Was a Man

Kelcey Parker Ervick

After The Narrative of Arthur Gordon Pym of Nantucket
by Edgar Allan Poe.

MEN WASH UP ON THE SHORE: DEAD, ALMOST DEAD, HUNGRY.

They all have stories. She thinks she has a story, too, even if she doesn't yet know what it is. Surely it has to do with the light. Not the absence of darkness, but the pure sliver of light that beams from the lighthouse into a sea of darkness. She thinks of the night sky like this sometimes: a sea of darkness. But if the sky is a sea, does that make the wild sea a sky? In daylight she can see the sea, and she calls it the sky. The boats with their winged sails fly across the sky. She and her aunt live alone at the edge of the wet, wet sky, beneath a starlit sea. How did she get here?

There once was a man from Nantucket.

Let's say his name was Arthur Gordon Pym. Let's say he wrote a narrative of his adventures at sea. That he left out very little about the parts of the ship, the geography of seas, the nature of his desperate and dehydrated dreams, the quantities and types of food available, the deaths of shipmates, the cannibalism, the encounters with savages, the cryptic markings on the chasm rocks, the escape, and the quality and texture of the air as he sailed toward the southernmost pole.

But he left out a lot of other things, this man from Nantucket. Let's say that just before these adventures, Arthur Gordon Pym knew a girl. That he got her up in a certain way. Not knowing what to do about the girl and her situation, he found himself overcome with strange desires. He became consumed by "visions of shipwreck and famine; of death and captivity among barbarian hordes." And so he left the girl and situation, and he hopped on a ship, the *Grampus*.

Be careful what you wish for, man from Nantucket.

Let's say the girl he knew gave birth to a girl. That the girl he knew died giving birth to a baby girl, and that this daughter, orphaned, was turned over to her aunt. Let's say that the aunt was a lighthouse keeper, one of the few women on the job.

Growing up at the edge of the sea, the girl reads. Not folktales, which seem filled with motherless girls like her. No, she reads of adventures on land and sea. She reads of Gulliver, Robinson Crusoe, King Arthur, Robin Hood, and Don Quixote. Her aunt's small house is filled with books that the men from the ships leave behind.

The girl imagines that the rocks that jut into the water are the bow of her ship that she sails into the seas. That she is headed on a seafaring adventure. When boats appear, they are coming toward her ship for help or to trade information. When supplies are low, she eyes her aunt's thick arms and neck like: food. That is what adventurers do.

Then again: she is the savage, the native, the heathen. On the wall of the lighthouse, she uses a rock to scratch stories and stick figures. She speaks her own language, worships the all-powerful lighthouse.

Men wash up on the shore: dead, almost dead, hungry.

From her books she knows the men will measure her, take note of her clothing, and inquire about her gods. She will point to the lighthouse; she will bow down before it. They will tell her about their God, the one with the capitalized G. He is in threes: father, son, holy spirit. Omnipotent, omnipresent, omniscient. Who is this amazing deity? she will ask. Where does he live? Why, he is everywhere, they will tell her. But I can't see him, she will say, frightened, for this God is too much like her own father, whom she has also never seen. She will run to the top of the lighthouse and scream and scream.

The men stay for a night or two, until the weather clears, until the ship is repaired, until the next ship appears. She follows the men so she can take things from their pockets and satchels. A magnifying glass, a compass, a book, a bottle of something that burns her throat when she drinks. To be a girl is to be not quite unseen—for the men see her, tell jokes about her girlness, predict her bland future—but rather to be invisible. As they laugh and say how many children she will have, what sort of husband, she searches their bags and pockets. She knows they are wrong about her future.

She spies scrimshaw. Confiscates it. Later she will rub her fingertips along the images on the whalebone, images of faces and fish, ships and seas she will never know. She steals a knife, which she keeps for the men who come too close, whose drunken eyes leer. She is not always so invisible.

When there are no men, she spends her days listening to the conch shell for its messages and whispering her secrets back into its pearled depths. She catches fish, names them, and eats them. Practice.

The girl grows and learns. She follows the aunt up, up, up the spiral steps, lugging buckets of whale oil, and torches the candles and polishes the lenses that cast the light into the darkness. The small flame magnified for miles. She practices each task and embraces the rhythm of up and down, light and darkness. She knows that others go to church to worship a capitalized God, but she enters her god and worships from within. When the aunt is gone, she carves more stories on its darkened walls.

The aunt doesn't believe in God anymore, not since He took away her husband and son. This was before the girl arrived, but not long before, and the aunt has forever connected the girl's arrival with their departures. *Devoted Husband*, it says on the larger tombstone behind the house. *Beloved Son*, reads the smaller one beside it, *Died March 6, 1827. Lived 1 y. 2 m. 9 d.*

In the sand at the foot of the lighthouse, the girl uses a stick to compose predictions for her tombstone. She tries out a series of dates for her death. Her birthdate stays the same in 1828, but her death date varies. Maybe it will be February 21, 1871. Or August 20, 1859. Or any of the thousands of days in between. Or after. Or even before. She tries out inscriptions: *Orphan Girl. Castaway. Cannibal. She Kept the Light.*

(In another version of the story, she would not spend her youth writing tombstone messages. She would have two parents and a sister to perform skits with. She would have her father's last name, not her aunt's husband's name. She would go to school and become a teacher or something.)

(In still another version, she would have been a boy. But actually that is not another version. That is another story altogether.)

Growing up, the daughter has two questions: Who is my mother? Who is my father? As to the former, the aunt says: My sister, God rest her soul. As to the latter, the aunt says nothing. The aunt slips up only once, without even knowing it, but that is all the daughter needs. The girl keeps the name of her father alight in her mind just as her aunt keeps the light on for the sailors. *Pym. Pym. Pym.*

The name is both foreign and familiar. There once was a man from Nantucket.

One night, the light burns out, a ship wrecks near their shore, and a man dies in the darkness. Did the aunt forget to add more oil? Did she do it on purpose? Either way, after that, the aunt turns. Becomes a different sort of aunt. She spends more time writing in the log book and increasingly leaves the lighthouse duties to the girl. The girl, who is beginning to think of herself as a woman, reads the aunt's log and instead of weather reports and accounts of the men who wash up, all is gloom: *Nothing but sorrow, without and within. This is not a fit place for anyone to live in. Oh, what a place. All misery and darkness. This is such a dreary place to be in all alone.*

All alone? If the aunt is all alone, that must make the girl all alone, too. She climbs to the top of the lighthouse and screams.

From the top of the lighthouse, the girl who is beginning to think of herself as a woman looks out to the sea and thinks about her father. *Pym.* Familiar, foreign. She can't place it. Nor can she dwell on it. The light is her duty now. The aunt is her duty now. If the light goes out the ships will run aground. Nights, she can't sleep, thinking about the light. She peers out her window to make sure it still glows. When she does sleep, her dreams are of the light. It is always dimming, always receding. She can't get to it in time. She cries out. *Pym!*

The aunt is raving mad when the men wash up on the shore. One man is dead, another is almost dead, a third is very hungry.

The girl, upon seeing the third, finds herself, despite her breakfast of cooked eggs, suddenly hungry, too. She is used to feeling love for the dead ones, whose puckered and bloated faces were like scrimshaw that told stories of their now-finished lives. She occasionally felt love for the almost-dead ones, if only because they gave her something to do other than lighthouse duties, such as bringing them water and blankets until the doctor arrived. But when they returned from almost-death and could speak again, they smelled rotten, and she could not love them anymore.

Is it love she feels for the hungry man? It is her nineteenth summer, and she longs to feel real love for a living man. She tests the idea, but it fails. No, she feels hunger.

It is late at night when she makes herself alone with him. They are under the moon that shines like a light on the night's dark sea. She cannot see that part of him, but she is hungry and she touches it. And when she does, she thinks of a lighthouse. Rising up between sea and sky, sky and sea. She lets go with her hand and then. She can feel the light in her darkness.

(In one version of the story, this is how she comes to have her own daughter. How, even years later when the chickens have been washed into the sea by a strong storm and there are no more eggs for her or her daughter to eat, she never feels hunger again.)

(In another version of the story, this is how she comes to leave the lighthouse. She calls her hunger love, and she follows the hungry man to the city, where she loves and hungers for her husband and children in quiet desperation; where, nights, she dreams of the light and stormy seas.)

In this version, the hungry man grows satiated by meals eaten with the babbling aunt, nights with the girl. But the girl's hunger only grows. She begins to fear it will never be satisfied. She wants the man, but he is not enough. She wants him to ask about her god, to learn her language, interpret her carvings.

Instead she says: Take me with you. Take me on an adventure at sea. I want shipwreck and famine, death and captivity!

The man laughs, and it is only then that she realizes she is nothing but a girl. Not even a savage. She has never been a savage, just a girl who nurses men back to life. Just a girl who keeps the light bright so the men can go on their adventures.

Still: the girl fears her hunger, her own savage nature. Maybe she will eat him.

One night she speaks the name of her father. Pym? the hungry man says. Pym, she says. Of Nantucket? he says. She doesn't know. I've heard his tale, he says. He has a tale? Tell me!

But the hungry man doesn't remember exactly. Something about mutiny and cannibals. Did he go to the center of the earth? the hungry man wonders aloud, gnawing on a chicken bone, but can't quite recollect. Is he alive? she asks, clutching the man's collar. The hungry man can't recall.

January 24, 1848. Hurricane Pym. Devoted daughter.

Whale oil costs more each day, and there are rumors of gold in California. The hungry man boards a ship, sets off on a new adventure. This is how the girl comes to understand the world and its workings. Men come, men go. Women stay put, women go mad. There once was a man, but now he is gone. This is something her mother could have told her if her mother had lived. Women give birth, women die.

After the man leaves, the girl paces and paces. He has a tale, he has a tale. If he has a tale, maybe she has a tale, maybe he wrote about her. Maybe he is alive, maybe she will find him. Inside the house, she takes one book after another from her aunt's shelves, tears them in two, tosses them in the fire. The aunt cries out. Where is it, the girl says. Where?

And then she sees it: *The Narrative of Arthur Gordon Pym of Nantucket.* Had it been there all along?

The seas cease, the birds silence, the aunt dissolves into nothing.

The girl reads.

Let's say you're a man from Nantucket and you've been at sea for months. You didn't have to go to sea at all; adventure just seemed more appealing. No one writes stories about a life at home with a woman and child. But that was before you saw your best friend die and had hunger so strong that you ate the flesh of your sacrificed shipmate. Now you're floating on a canoe, headed toward the South Pole, where you've heard tell of an entrance to an inner world and a superior society, and although this sounds fantastic, as in impossible and improbable, you have just seen your two dozen shipmates swallowed by a trap set in the earth by savages, and you barely made it off the island alive, and you are with Peters, the only other survivor, and a native named Nu-Nu who is now dead in your canoe, and you're desperate enough to believe in the wildest story.

Now let's say you are a girl reading this story about a man from Nantucket, and all you can think is: Papa? Is that what I would I call you? And: Afterward, in all those years, did you try to find me, Papa?

But her father's story ends before it is actually over (like everything, everything), and no one knows if he made it to the center of the earth, and it doesn't matter anyway because by then she knows he did not write about her, did not try to find her, probably never thought about her or her mother at all, and she feels the clay of her heart harden. She sets down the book to tend the light. These are the only things she can rely on: darkness, herself. When she returns to the chair and reads in the epilogue about the death of Pym, she is not surprised and is only slightly moved to know he was alive for the first decade of her life.

The girl is a woman now, mentally and emotionally. She has long been a woman physically. She logs her days: the storms, the ships that wreck, the household maintenance, the crabs torn apart by gulls. Sometimes she adds something else in the log, something that has nothing to do with the weather or ship traffic, but there is no one to notice it. She comes to understand her father's writing, her aunt's writing, even the inscrutable symbols of the savages in her father's book: some things get written down, some omitted, some forgotten; others kept deep within. Etched in sand, scratched on scrimshaw.

There once was a man from Nantucket. This is the story of his forgotten daughter.

Gulls and tides. Sometimes you just want quiet. Inside, the house is cold. Sometimes she reads aloud when the aunt, in a moment of lucidity, requests it. She reads *The Narrative of Arthur Gordon Pym of Nantucket*. It always ends the same, with her father sailing toward the South Pole where he sees the large, shrouded white figure. The girl makes up her own final lines in her father's voice: "And as I gazed at the figure, I knew it was the woman I left behind, holding our daughter in her arms. At last I was returning to them."

But that, she knows, is her own version of the story, not his.

Meanwhile, men still wash up on the shore: dead, almost dead, hungry. The girl keeps a pilfered gun strapped to her leg.

One day there is a Negro. He washes up on the shore alone with a broken boat. He is gaunt, hunched over, and she does not know at first if he is dead, almost dead, or hungry. It is 1851. She knows she should turn him in. She knows she shouldn't. In her father's book, the dark-skinned men are called savages. The new law calls them fugitives.

(In one version of the story, she tricks him into staying long enough that she can alert officials of the nearby town and turn him in. She collects a reward and wonders what to do with it.)

But this is not that version, and this is not her father's book. For when she looks into the man's eyes, with the lighthouse reflecting in them, she understands that he is on an adventure. She gives him food and points him toward the city she's never seen. He thanks her with a voice from the far-away seas, as deep as the skies.

The aunt dies. The girl digs the grave herself, writes in the fresh earth with a stick—just one word, *AUNT*—and stabs the stick in the ground.

Some days she thinks of the Negro and hopes he got where he was going. Some days she thinks where he was going might also be bad for him, that he will encounter savages. She wonders if there is anywhere on this earth he can go.

Other days she thinks of the hungry man, who devoured her so long ago.

There once was a man. She should have eaten him.

Her father had not written about her, not in his famous narrative, anyway. She wishes the savages had killed him with the rest. Then he wouldn't have written anything at all.

Often she wonders, what if she didn't light the light? All the men in the world would wash up on her dark shore. She would set a trap and kill them all.

March 6, 1900. Eater of men.

The older she gets, the more she thinks of her girlhood when she believed she was a savage. She makes mandalas out of shells in the sand. Or forms the shells into large letters, words for the birds to carry into the clouds.

She puts a message in a bottle, tosses the bottle in the sea. The waves roll it back to her. The sky is the sea, the sea is the sky.

In the log book she makes up words, phrases, even letters. She sketches symbols like the savages in her father's story.

Let's say it's your job to decipher, to tell the story of the woman who kept the light. Surely she has one.

May 7, 2075. Oldest Woman in the World.

Tonight there are such gales. The gales will bring more men: dead, almost dead, hungry. But for now, no one arrives, and supplies are running low. She can't see any stars. The entire world is house, tower, sand, sea. She takes her father's book and climbs to the top of the lighthouse. She lights the wick, tears out a page of the book, and touches it to the flame. She dips another page in whale oil and lights it, startled by its fury. She lights another. The fiery pages gather at her feet, and, although she is burning the evidence, wants it turned to ash, there is something she can no longer ignore. For years she has believed the book was her father's story, but now, as its pages catch the hem of her dress on fire, she confronts an idea she has resisted for years: that her father never existed at all.

That there never was a man from Nantucket. That he was only ever a story.

And if that is true (for it is), what does that make her?

Alone at the top of the fiery lighthouse, she screams and screams.

Somewhere in the distant sea, there is a man on a ship who sees an unusually bright light on the shore. It fills him with hunger.

KELCEY PARKER ERVICK spent many summers visiting her grandparents in Barnegat, New Jersey, gazing out at Old Barney, the distinctive red-and-white lighthouse across the bay. Some of the details and journal entries in her story are taken from *Women Who Kept the Lights: An Illustrated History of Female Lighthouse Keepers* by Mary Louise Clifford and J. Candace Clifford, which she found at her grandparents' house and "borrowed" with a promise to write a story one day. She lives in South Bend, Indiana, an hour away from Michigan City Lighthouse, where Harriet Colfax kept the light for forty-three years. She is pretty sure women lighthouse keepers are the most adventurous of us all.

10

THE LEGENDS OF ŻORRO

Michael Czyzniejewski

BEFORE MY GRANDFATHER DIED, HE REVEALED TO ME THAT WHEN he was a young man in the 1950s, he led a double life as the masked vigilante known as Żorro—not *Zorro*, but Żorro, with a hard Z, like in "vision," "garage," or "Zsa Zsa Gabor." When my grandfather revealed this, he was taking a lot of pills, maybe not making a lot of, if any, sense. The more his health declined, the more Grandpa insisted he fought crime all up and down Milwaukee Avenue, wearing a red-and-white version of Zorro's black costume, including a vest smattered with red sequins. When I told him he was full of shit—Grandpa was the first adult to whom I could openly swear—he journeyed further into detail, regaling me with tales of the break-ins, pick-pocketings, and purse snatchings he'd halted with his trusty rapier. I'd call bullshit again, and he'd smile and say something like, "What do you know, you kielbasa?" and that would be that. At least until the next day, when he'd start again, more and more adamant that he was Żorro, scourge of the Chicago Polish underworld.

This was before we had anything like the internet to verify a sickly old man's tales. When I wanted to know something, I'd look it up in the *World Book* encyclopedias in the public library. Since the *World Book* didn't have information on local superheroes, I resorted to my last resort: adults.

First I asked my mom if she ever saw her dad use a sword, if he was an accomplished fencer. She didn't answer until I asked twice, and then she just looked at me as if I'd asked her to toss me a beer. I went to ask my dad in the garage, where he spent his nights listening to hippie music, drinking Old Styles, and flipping through the *Playboys* he didn't think I knew about. I went for the more point-blank route with him, asking, "Did Grandpa ever dress up like a Polish Zorro and fight crime?" Dad laughed at this, but when I said I was serious, he closed the garage door, looked around as if someone was listening, and whispered in my ear: "Now you know the truth, son. Your granddad was the Polish Zorro. And I'm the Polish Lone Ranger. Your mom the Polish Wonder Woman. And you, you're the Polish Sausage!"

I didn't appreciate being mocked—I was thirteen, so of course—but Dad was right: Grandpa dressing up as a disco superhero and sword-fighting crime was as likely as the Cubs winning the World Series, but a gabillion times more ridiculous. Grandpa retired from Inland Steel, smoked Dutch Masters, and could fart on command, his superpower. It wasn't in his profile, swashbuckling.

That's how I spent that summer, going to my grandparents', wondering if Grandpa would bring up all this Żorro nonsense, which he always did. At 1:20, we'd watch the Cubs. Grandma would cook something with cabbage in it, adding to their house's permanent cabbage stench. More often than not, the Cubs would get shellacked—this was 1983, the year before that Sandberg team—and at least once a game, Grandpa would lift his leg, let one fly, and say something like, "That one sounded good coming off the bat." Then he'd nod off and I'd have to field his stink. Grandma would come into the TV room, wake him with pills every couple of innings, sometimes his insulin. Today, I know my mom sent me there *because* he was dying, that she wanted me to get to know him, but I don't think I knew that then. I was there to watch the game, and when it was over, go home.

That didn't make for a particularly fun summer, watching bad baseball with my sick grandpa and eating *gołabki* until I, too, smelled like a cabbage and farted like a pack of firecrackers. Summers prior, I played Little League, but I'd gotten worse and worse every season, a typical two-inning kid, the minimum the coach was mandated to play everybody. In 1983, I was supposed to move on to Babe Ruth, to the full-size field, which I wanted no part of, not with my puss arm and the increasing terror I'd get hit in the face by a pitch. When the sign-up day approached, I prayed my dad would forget, and maybe I'd prayed hard enough, because he did. I thought this would free me up to spend my hot afternoons at the city pool, staring at high school girls in their bathing suits and jumping off the low dive and splashing around like an idiot, things at which I genuinely excelled. But then my mom read a story about a kid in Wichita who got polio—in 1982—from swimming at a public pool, losing the use of his legs. I'd had my shots, I explained, told Mom that polio had been cured, but she would have none of it, said this could be a new strain, something Salk hadn't seen. Unless I wanted to end up like FDR, she declared my swimming days over.

I didn't have a lot of friends, either, which is what happened when you quit sports and your mom phoned every other mom in your class and told them about the Wichita kid, leading to pool bans for most Holy Trinity eighth graders, gutting my popularity to an all-time low. My grandma and grandpa's house, complete with cabbage and the Cubs, became my go-to option.

That was also the summer that the neighborhood started to change, that most of the signs at the stores switched from Polish to English. Iron bars striped a lot of windows, metal accordion gates barricaded doors. Father Casimir at Holy Trinity died from a stroke, and instead of replacing him with another old Polack from the neighborhood, the archdiocese put in a Filipino guy named Father David, who didn't speak Polish or even English all that well—at least he was nice to us altar boys, not caring if we wore gym shoes to mass or had hair below our ears. The 9:30 Sunday Polish mass was canceled, too, causing more than one family to transfer to St. Viator's or St. Ed's. This opened slots to a lot of non-Polish kids, some of whom weren't even Catholic, the local CPS so shitty, their parents would rather go parochial than trust the city with their children's futures.

To make it to my grandparents' for first pitch, I'd get up around ten, eat cereal while watching game shows—*Sale of the Century* was my thing—then I'd ride the L two stops to Western and walk five blocks to that cabbage-reeking slab on Shakespeare Avenue. I'd been making that trip alone since I was ten, no thought to it ever being a bad idea for a kid to travel that far through the city by himself. My mom trained me to stand on the train so no one would sit next to me. The whole trip took less than ten minutes; if I kept to myself, I'd be fine. I could see Grandma and Grandpa's roof from the L platform, then it was a straight shot across the Milwaukee and Armitage intersection to their front door. I never went at night, never on the weekends.

That summer I also started to get harassed, around the Western station and on my walk toward Shakespeare. There was the expected stuff, winos who usually ignored me but for some reason began asking for change. I was pretty sure the woman always smoking outside the Brown's Chicken was a prostitute, but she might have been waiting for a bus. Danger lurked, but I survived.

The real problem was the older kids—kids I didn't recognize from school—kids who started to give me shit. Someone hearing this story might assume these kids were a "gang," if you could call four or five teenagers on dirt bikes a gang. I'd get off the train, cross the big intersection, and there they'd be, circling like a pack of wolves. Sometimes, they'd pop wheelies, sometimes all the way down the street. Other times they'd have a ramp rigged up on the sidewalk, a piece of propped-up plywood that launched them an inch or two off the ground with each jump. Despite the fact I feared them, these jumps made them godlike, men among boys, kings among men. I wasn't allowed to do tricks at home, no wheelies, no jumps, not even riding too fast. These kids were like a squadron of James Deans, the coolest kids I'd ever encountered.

My only mistake was having the audacity to stop and watch, knowing these were the same kids who threw garbage at me and used profanity I'd never heard before. Still, I thought their bike stunts the most awesome thing in the world, and if I melted down to a skeleton by looking at the celestial glories inside the Ark, then so be it. Before long, one of them noticed me watching them and asked me who the hell I was. I told them *Dzien dobry* and explained that my grandparents lived around the corner, that I was on my way to catch the Cubs with my grandpa. I asked if they were Cubs fans, and when they didn't say anything, I asked if they were Polish. At that, another kid jumped off his bike, walked up to me, and pushed me backward on my ass, sending a jolt into my tailbone and up my spine. Then he hocked a loogie on my chest and all the other kids laughed. Suddenly, I had the distinct feeling these guys weren't going to be my new best friends, let alone give me a turn on their ramp: They were most likely White Sox fans and not at all of the Polish persuasion.

Because summer was almost half over, and I hadn't hung out with a single person anywhere near my own age, I stood up and blurted out that I had a new Schwinn Predator and that it was orange and chrome and I thought their ramp was cool. The kid who'd spat on me made a move like he was going to do something worse, but another kid, the tallest of the group, the one with the longest hair and a shadow of a mustache forming on his lip, stopped him and said to me, "Do you think you can take our ramp, tough guy?"

I peeked at the ramp. A stack of three bricks and a piece of pressboard formed a ten-degree angle off the sidewalk, an engineering masterpiece.

"I can take it," I said, and for some reason added, "I can take it *hard*."

All the guys *oohed* and *aahed*. The mustachioed leader said, "Okay, make it happen."

It was already after one and I had to get to my grandparents' before they called home, wondering where I was. I told the kids that it'd have to be tomorrow, that I didn't have my bike—which was obvious—and the game would start soon. They all laughed again, one of the other kids calling me a baby. Another yelled, "Cubs suck!" The leader told them to shut up and said I was cool. "He's cool," he said, just like that. "He's going to show us tomorrow, right, Ace?"

I nodded, said, "Shit yeah. Tomorrow."

Then the five of them rode off, leaving the ramp behind, as if they owned that neighborhood, that they could construct major dirt bike obstacles and leave them wherever they wanted, confident no one would mess with their business. I jogged to my grandparents' house, making it just in time, but I couldn't wait until the next day, when I'd show those older boys who they were dealing with, the Polish Ramp-Jumping Prince of Chicago.

Of course, that's not how it went down. First of all, I wasn't even allowed to take my bike that far from home and had to wait for my mom to go to the bathroom so I could sneak it out of the garage. I rode up Western under the L tracks, pedaling as fast as I could. I could see the gang of boys from across the intersection, their ramp set up on the other side of the street, but they hadn't seen me yet. I waited for the light, sped toward them, and without hesitating, passed two of the guys in the ramp line, hit the pressboard at full speed and took off. At most, I got two inches off the ground, landing maybe five inches beyond take-off—I'd been picturing something else, much more lift, E.T. and Elliott crossing the moon. But still, I thought how I'd handled it all—cutting in line, taking off without clearance—was me paying my admission. When I landed, I spun around, skidding my back tire along the sidewalk, facing my new peers.

"And that's how you do *that*," I said.

Without applauding, without cheering, the assholes converged on me, knocking me over, then ripping my Predator out from between my legs, dragging the chain across my calf, tearing both skin and tube sock en route. They considered my bike—for what it's worth, they seemed impressed—and for a minute, they argued over who would get it. I thought they were discussing who would get the first turn to ride it, and even though my parents forbade sharing, I was going to let them: it's what friends were for. I tried to explain how they could all get a turn, and the loogie kid from the day before put his foot on my chest, keeping me on my back like a manic turtle. When I explained that I really needed my bike, that I needed to get going to my grandparents' house, Loogie let me up, even pulled me to my feet, then punched me right in the eye, really, really hard. It was the first time I'd ever been punched in the face, and I did not like it.

At this point, it was clear these guys were stealing my bike, that they'd set me up for it. I thought for sure the leader kid with the faint mustache was going to take it for himself. Instead, they took a pack approach and assessed who had the shittiest ride. It was determined that this shrimpy kid with braces had the worst bike, a white Huffy with a cushioned banana seat covered in duct tape. The leader kid awarded this guy my Predator, and Braces mounted and rode off, the other boys following, all of them giving me the finger as they disappeared. Just like that, my new Predator belonged to him and not me. His crappy old Huffy with the stupid seat was suddenly my bike, lying on the sidewalk like a discarded corpse.

Grandma covered her mouth when she saw me walking up Shakespeare. She took me inside to the bathroom and showed me my face: my eye was yellow and purple and swollen like I had a balloon under my cheek. She took a piece of raw steak out of the refrigerator and made me hold it over my eye, then sat me down in the breakfast nook, torturing me into telling her what'd happened. At first, I told her that I fell on the train and hit my eye on a window, which she didn't believe. Next I told her I fell while jumping ramps with my bike and slammed my face against a tree root. She asked me where my bike was, and I said that it happened that morning, before I left home, that my bike was safe in our garage. She said there was no way my mother would have sent me to her house with an eye like that, not on the train, not alone. I told her I didn't want to tell her what really happened, so she pinched me on the wrist, which she knew would make me do or say anything. I flat-out squealed, every detail about the gang—yes, *gang*—the setup, the punch, the little shit in the braces riding off and leaving me his crappy Huffy. Grandma pinched my wrist twice more for saying "shit" and "crappy" and asked where the kid's bike was. I told her that I left it by the ramp, that it was really crappy—another pinch—but it didn't matter because my parents were going to kill me. She then patted me on the butt and sent me and my steak into the TV room with Grandpa. Already, the Cubs were losing 1–0, and Grandpa had dozed off in his chair. I sat and watched with the piece of sirloin on my face but fell asleep, sucking in the urge to cry, beef blood dripping down my cheek.

I woke some time later to shouting. The score flashed on the TV screen—the Cubs were losing 5–1 in the top of the fifth inning. I thought the shouting was about the score, but I looked over at Grandpa's chair and it was empty. I got up, the steak falling from my lap to the sculpted carpet, and investigated where the yelling was coming from. In the main hallway, the attic stairs were hanging down. I tried to spy what was up there—I'd never been—but could only see darkness. As I made my way to the kitchen, I determined it was my grandparents who were screaming at each other, Grandma repeating, louder each time, "Absolutely not. Absolutely not." Grandpa said something about getting out of his way, and Grandma said again, "Absolutely not."

I entered the kitchen and froze. My grandmother was blocking the back door, blocking it from Żorro.

Goddamn, I thought.

Grandpa's outfit was exactly like he'd described: white pants, white blousy shirt, and a red sequined vest that threw the light from the ceiling fixture all around the room like a pile of rubies. On his head sat a Zorro-like hat, the flat kind with the huge brim, also covered in red sequins, topping a red headscarf that came down over Grandpa's eyes, two holes bored out so he could see. On his feet he wore knee-high red leather boots, and dangling from his hip, a sword, shiny silver and as long as me. Hung over one of the chairs at the breakfast table was a cape, bright red with a white Polish eagle emblazoned on the back.

My grandfather, Żorro, insisted my grandmother move, claiming there was great injustice that needed justifying. He would duck one way and she'd counter, then parry the other and she'd do the same. Grandpa, it seemed, couldn't outmaneuver his wife, surprisingly spry, let alone right any wrongs.

"Wally needs his bike back," Grandpa said. "And you know and I know who this is a job for."

I stood in disbelief as the two danced, still in shock over the fact that Żorro existed. Perhaps just as unbelievable, the costume still fit—even in his prime, Grandpa must have been pudgy and kind of hunched over. Nevertheless, he looked dashing, a sense of justice mingling in the air with a hint of sauerkraut.

At least until Grandpa drew his sword. That's when things got really messy. Grandma lunged forward, grabbing at Grandpa's arm, and Grandpa—what he was thinking, I don't know—sidestepped her, pulling the sword back so she couldn't grab it. First the curtains fell, the sword slashing them from the rod, sending an aura of light into the room, across the plentitude of sequins, bathing the room in red. Then the sword's tip, glistening in the new light, stabbed me square in the palm of my right hand (I probably blocked it from hitting my face), leaving a dot of red, a dot that quickly grew to a steady blood flow. When Grandpa realized what he'd done, he dropped the sword, pulled off his hat and mask, and helped Grandma pull me to the sink. Grandma rinsed the wound under the faucet, blood mixing the water to pink as it circled the drain. Grandpa fetched the Bactine and some cotton balls from the bathroom and stood ready, his complexion invisible, his face telling me he'd never regretted anything more his whole life. When Grandma was convinced the blood had stopped, she doused me with the Bactine—burning like a thousand hells—and bandaged me up.

I ate a bowl of walnut ice cream as Grandma helped Grandpa out of his Żorro uniform and back into his slacks and flannel shirt. Grandpa was still shaken, if not shaking, and kept apologizing with each piece of his bad-ass costume peeled from his pruney, pale skin. I was still stunned, both from the reality of Żorro and the fact I'd just been stabbed, yet I didn't feel any pain, let alone anger. I felt terrible for doubting him and told him so, but he said it was okay, said we were even for him stabbing me—then he winked. Blood covered everything, and Grandma sopped it up with a sponge and bucket. Then she put the Żorro getup back in a dry-cleaner bag, replacing it and the sword in the attic. Grandpa and I spent the rest of the day watching the end of the Cub game—they came back and won 7–6—and I asked him to tell me all the stories of Żorro again, but to go slowly, to not skip any details.

In the meantime, Grandma said she had to run out for more sponges and bandages, but when she came back, she had my Predator. The short kid with the braces had just moved to the end of their block, and his mother was volunteering with my grandma at the Holy Trinity rectory. Grandma went to their house, explained what had happened, and the mother immediately returned my plundered bike.

"She really let that little shit have it as I was leaving," Grandma said.

"Good," I said.

"Good," Grandpa said.

I ate dinner at their house that night, pork chops in sour cream, giving the wound on my hand time to close. Grandma took off the bandages, sprayed it again with Bactine, and covered it with two Band-Aids, which I would explain away with a weeding injury, something my mom would buy, Grandma always sending me out to the yard. Grandma told me to never bring my bike to her house again, to ride it only where I was allowed. I also swore to stay off ramps and away from strange boys and to pray to the Lady of Czestochowa every night. Grandma called ahead to my parents, concocted a story about the attic stairs falling down, the corner catching me in the eye, that they should press more beef into it as soon as I walked in the door.

"Dziękuję, Busia," I said. I called her my hero.

"Kocham cie, Waltek."

I rode home, by myself, in the loud, endless darkness, unable to pedal fast enough.

My grandpa died soon after that, over the All-Star break, and my time at the house on Shakespeare turned into helping to pack and clean, Grandma moving in with us, into the spare room next to mine. Most of the boys who stole my bike, including Braces and Mustache, showed up at Holy Trinity for eighth grade—Braces and I were best friends by Christmas—though nobody ever brought up the Predator incident. The next summer, the Cubs won the East, Mom let me get a pool pass again, and

I prepped for high school at Quigley South. There was also a new box up in my closet, one that was big and long and taped tight and had "Baseball Cards for Wally" written on the side in Magic Marker. I couldn't open it, Grandma said, not until I was older, and never in front of my mom or dad. It would be a while, I knew, but I felt comfort in its presence, knowing it was all real, justice on hold until I was worthy of donning everything inside.

MICHAEL CZYZNIEJEWSKI's most recent collection of stories is *I Will Love You for the Rest of My Life: Breakup Stories*. He is Associate Professor of English at Missouri State University, where he serves as editor in chief of *Moon City Review* and managing and literary editor for Moon City Press.

11

THE WONDERWORLD

or

*A Ship Has Many Secrets, More than Any Late
Consumptive Usher to a Grammar School Might Know*

Margaret Patton Chapman

After Moby Dick.

Two or three years ago there was a great run on female sailors. Every
newspaper has its paragraph announcing the discovery of a female sailor.
The result was a thorough conviction in the public mind that all sailors
were female sailors—that there were no other sailors than female sailors
in disguise; and now the curiosity would be the discovery of a male sailor, if
such a phenomenon could be well authenticated.

—*The Examiner*, Boston, March 25, 1843

I WAS A YOUNG MAN ONCE, WHEN I WENT TO SEA.

O! It was miles and miles of salt drudgery, hemmed in by wooden rails
and monstrous depths. I was hired as a cooper's assistant on a great New
Bedford whaler, an ill-fated venture, three years from port. And it was
fearsome, yes, a hundred frights in a thousand sunsets, and one in ten the

night with no sleep at all for the fear of meeting death in it, of waking in water or worse. A thousand days of hiding, too—pissing in buckets where no one could see, buckets I made for the purpose, and washing in those same buckets secret bloody rags. Still it invites me, even now, that watery world which laps outside my window, which whispers me to sleep, which sings to me with the lonesome tenor of the beloved and the drowned.

Granny!—sailors call me as they stumble in off the street, a half dozen sea rats in monkey jackets and patched woolen trousers, beards natty with salt and spray, with their rough-and-tumble jumble of land-leery, marked-up limbs. *Come here!*—they call out—*Bring us some beer!*

Little know they that this stoop-ed woman, this crook-ed, cloak-ed crone—were I to undo my buttons, push up my sleeves, I, too, could display my scrimshawed skin! There are lines on me, faded blue India ink on this old bag—distortions, new monsters made on me, yes!—where the whalehead Leviathan, the harpooner, and the crude ship come together in a menagerie of weird chimera that I transform as I move. And the names, the names upon my folded flesh, those men I keep beneath my lace and linen. My late husband—so recently late—saw, but none else. Not for some time. There are men whose lives I hide in my underclothes that would shock the young sailors who come to this place. These call me Granny and laugh at my crackled voice and call their friends to come listen how I curse them in my frailty, my tall leanness sunk down, my long body doubled over, hidden under chemise and skirt and shawl and cap and the hundred other undeserved encumbrances of age.

When I was a young man at sea, we sailed to the southern realms past the edges of the equator, and I wore a vest and trousers cut at the knee, and the sun browned my shoulders, and my arms rippled with muscle, shining wet in that sun, and the ship and men and the whale were a deep black story, not a memory faded blue. I remember pulling rope as sunlight sparkled from the wave tips, how my hands were rough callused, and the hemp was heavy and thick with that rhythm, that heave-ho among us, how we all, all us men and boys, our arms the coupling rods, around and pull, around and pull, three dozen limbs in motion—how perfect we were!—all our shades of brown darkening into black, all our ink-ed arms, and how, then, you stood behind me in the pull of it, in the lean back of it, and when the line of men fell back like dominoes with the rope, how I fell back against you, and the crossover of arms in the pulling, in the sweat, the sweet sweat of youth. O! To be young in a line of men again, as our arms cross and bodies lean in to one another. In my memory, it is a task never ending, and the thing we heave up is nothing but an agreeable infinity of heavy rope.

Here, Granny!—one young one calls out now, and raises a row from the group, arms up, saluting the casks—*Old Granny, fetch me another!* And they bang the table till it threatens to break to splinters, and I call out in my cackle—*patience, you little cunts!*—and they roar in laughter that sends one into a coughing fit ending only when he spits something foul and brown onto his hand and wipes it on his pant leg, leaving a greasy stripe.

They've come in from the sea, salted, browned and blacked, unsure of land, and sit at the table as they would on the ship, with the self-same seamen they have spent a month or six, they come in to drink my good ale and another and another, and they call me Granny and I curse them—*slow down, you buggers, slow down, there is no hurry, you fetid rats*—and they laugh at the blue old Granny: how slow she pours, how hobbled her walking, how she brings the mugs one at a time, then falls back behind the barrels to become invisible until they want another round.

In their chatter I hear the one with the greasy leg talk about a ship taken by a storm a few weeks hence, how the cousin of one of their crew is now known to be lost. They talk about ships wrecked, each tells a story, one worse than the next, of falterings and stavings-in and groundings and so many sailors lost at sea going back to the days of whalers, old and golden days to these young men, of ships out for years and making men rich. Ha! What riches did I find, save one, and that one secret, and beloved, and drowned.

Still, old sailors who stay on land love to talk like this, and young sailors, too—young sailors who, unlike you, do not yet know that they, too, can die.

O! What they do not know. They do not know—as I listen to their sea chatter, as I perch out of sight, as I fold this old body down into my clothes like the pelican folds into her wings—that I was a young man once, when I went to sea.

Margaret Patton Chapman is the author of the novella *Bell and Bargain* from Rose Metal Press. Her short fiction has appeared in *Diagram*, *The Collagist*, and *Prick of the Spindle*, among others. She lives in Durham, North Carolina, and teaches at Elon University.

12

My Name Was Never Frankenstein

Rachel Brittain

We are unfashioned creatures, but half made up . . .
—Mary Shelley, *Frankenstein*

WE WERE ON A SHIP, AS WAS USUAL FOR US IN THOSE DAYS. ANN, my lady's maid, was with me, not because I needed a lady's maid but because while I rarely kept with propriety, there were some customs I simply couldn't eschew without causing undue concern. And a young woman of three and twenty was never to travel alone—even if she was on a quest of redemption. Or so Ann had told me when I suggested she might stay behind.

"I will not," she said, putting on her most affronted tone. "I'm a proper Englishwoman."

"Well, I am neither of those things," I said, hoisting my skirt above my ankles and marching up the gangplank of the *Stirling*, Ann almost treading my hem, as the captain walked out to greet us.

The captain, a certain Daniel McRae, was wary of taking us on—two young ladies of proper standing—because this was no pleasure cruise or cross-channel journey. Captain McRae and his crew were setting out for the Arctic. As this was precisely my intended destination, and as I had enough coin to allay his concern, I was able to make a convincing argument in our favor.

"Hope you don't mind the cold, lass," McRae told me in his Scottish brogue. He was a stocky man, no taller than myself, with a full gray beard. He enlisted several of his crew to help with our trunks and led us down to the room that was to be ours, a small and understated affair down the companionway and near enough to the captain's quarters that we could "shout should there be any trouble."

Trouble, I knew, was more than likely on such a voyage. Still, I didn't hesitate to cross the threshold. I was decided on my choice, and though the room was small, the journey long, and the waters rough, there could be no turning back.

Ann couldn't help reminding me, again, that this wasn't entirely true—it wasn't really too late to turn back until we crossed the Arctic Circle and made port for the last time in Norway. Though this was not our first such journey, Ann had a tendency toward seasickness that never could be well managed and a certain reluctance to go along with my schemes that was likely borne more from concern for me than from any real decorum on her part.

"Once again into the icy waters," she said. "I do look forward to the day when you tire of life at sea."

I smiled and shook my head good-naturedly. She knew as well as I that only one thing would put a stop to my journeying, and that thing wasn't likely to be found sitting at home, twiddling my thumbs by the fireside.

"The captain seems decent enough," I said to ease her worries.

"Rather of a dizzy age, though," she said, unlatching our trunks to begin unpacking. There was no armoire and little furniture beside the bunked beds and a single desk and chair, but my maps and papers might be put away, at least.

"Oh, hush," I said without any real feeling behind it. I pulled out the handful of books I'd allowed myself for the journey and swatted her hand away as she tried to take them from me. "His age has no bearing on it."

"And yet . . ."

"Unless you intend to make a husband of him—and with your distaste for seafaring, I wouldn't recommend it—I think you'll find him perfectly capable of seeing us to the North and back."

She grumbled, and I realized I had inadvertently led us back to the very point I had been attempting to distract from. We finished arranging the room in unsettled silence.

The ship departed port in early afternoon, and by the time Ann and I returned below deck to make ourselves ready for supper with the captain, the sun was already sinking across the horizon.

Ann insisted on taking my hair out of its customary braid and pinning it up. Her steady fingers pulled gently, untangling knots and smoothing curls. She made quick work of it, twisting my honey-gold locks into a knot at the base of my neck, with a few curls loose at my ears. Ann turned me by the shoulders to examine me, smoothing my hair one last time and straightening the collar of my blouse before announcing me presentable.

"Will you tell him why you're truly here? What you're after?" she asked, tucking an errant strand of hair behind her own ear. I was quiet. "Lilibet, it's not just your secret to keep if—"

"It is my secret," I said, more sharply than I intended. I turned to hide the darkening expression on my face, pretending to adjust the creases of my blouse where it tucked into the band of my skirt. "It's my life and my business."

"And if it puts everyone else at risk?" she asked. The skin at her collarbone was flushed, and I could tell she was preparing for a row. I deflated, hands falling limply into my lap.

"I don't want to fight," I said.

Ann sighed. "Is that why we never talk about this?"

"Ann, please . . ."

"All right," she said finally. "But I'm not pretending to think it's a good idea. And if I'm asked directly, I won't lie."

Her face was set and the hard lines of her jaw pulled tight. I knew she meant what she said, but I also knew she would skirt the truth to the point of dishonesty to protect me, no matter her morals. The knowledge twisted deep in my stomach.

I smiled through the guilt and gave her a peck on the cheek. "I'd never ask you to," I told her.

↓

Captain McRae's cabin spanned the full width of the ship with large, square windows lining the aft. The last rays of evening sun glinted through them, refracting lines of rosy-orange light across the paneled floor. A large desk set with journals and precariously stacked books sat in front of the windows. To the left, a leather sofa was set off by two floor-to-ceiling bookshelves and to the right, a round table with three place settings.

The captain was a gracious host, welcoming us eagerly to his table, which was piled high with food—pigeon and bread and venison pie and all manner of pastries as well as several bottles of a purple claret. All unusually good fare for having just left port and not yet supplemented with hardtack, though I knew at sea it was only a matter of time.

"You seem comfortable with life on a ship, Miss Lavenza," Captain McRae said later, once our plates had all been cleared twice over. We were all full and awash in the pleasant warmth of wine.

"I spent a good deal of time at sea as a child," I told him.

"Aye, did you now?" he asked, though clearly unsurprised.

The question was meant to have an answer, and I saw the need to elaborate, though a part of me felt the less he knew the better. Still, there were parts of my story I could tell. After all the captain's kindness, surely he deserved to know that much at least. I poked at my pudding thoughtfully, not noticing the lengthening silence. A heeled boot pressed down on my own underneath the table. I glanced up, but Ann was looking studiously away.

"Ah, yes," I said to the captain, attempting to look composed. "When I was a girl, my mother and I came to England. She had a cousin there, a navy man turned merchant, and after my mother passed I spent several years at sea under his care."

"That seems rather unconventional," he said without any real judgment. So few people would do so, and I felt a surge of affection that I immediately attempted to tamp down.

"Perhaps," I said. "But better than becoming a foundling, I think."

McRae took a bite of his sponge cake before turning his attention to Ann, much to my relief. "And you were on this ship as well, lass?"

Ann's forehead crinkled. "No, thank heavens," she said. "We were united some years later in London, after Miss Lavenza's uncle realized that a ship wasn't the best place to raise a young lady."

This was something of a skirting of the truth, but one for which I knew Ann felt little guilt. Rather, my uncle had grown tired of me, his growing charge, and sent me back to the mainland until such an age as I could be married off. He died before that could happen, however, leaving me, his only living relative, as heir to a sizable estate.

Scratching his beard, the captain seemed to consider his next question before asking it. "And might I be so bold as to ask what brings two young ladies such as yourselves to my ship?"

I sipped my wine. This was one of a host of questions I had prepared myself for, though I didn't welcome it. "I'm looking for someone," I said.

The captain frowned (as did Ann, though, true to her word, she didn't say anything). "And you believe this someone might be on my ship?"

I shook my head over the rim of my glass, not quite laughing but a little amused at the thought. "I rather doubt it."

"Then you might be out of luck, lass. Not much to be found aside from ice and bears where we're headed."

I chose my next words carefully. "I have reason to believe that the one I'm looking for has been hiding in the Arctic," I said, and I could tell from his expression that he found my answers frustratingly vague. There were things I could not tell—would not tell—to a stranger, things I rarely even spoke of with Ann.

"You're more likely to find a body than anything else if he's been there long, I'm afraid. Those parts have claimed more souls than I'd care to count," he said.

"This soul would not be so easily claimed," I said darkly. Ann was staring at her plate next to me. The captain was clearly the probing type, and though I was loathe to say more, it seemed there was to be no escape. Fine: I would give him the bare details—the story in broad strokes—nothing more.

I swallowed, making up my mind. "Have you heard of the work of a Dr. Frankenstein, Captain?"

My throat closed over the name, but he didn't seem to notice. The captain shook his head. "Can't say that I have."

I licked my lips, which felt suddenly dry against my tongue. I took another sip of wine. "He was a man of science at the University of Ingolstadt," I explained. "Prussia. He was interested in physiology, biology, the science of life. He wanted to discover a way to animate the inanimate—to bring the dead to life."

Aside from the groaning of the ship and the muted sounds of the crew overhead, the room was quiet. When I didn't continue, the captain prompted me. "And did he?"

I closed my eyes briefly, feeling a deep ache in my chest that spoke of a desire to leave this conversation and this room. But these were the facts, and I could speak of facts surely, if nothing else. "He created *something*," I allowed. My voice came out quiet and dry, but I steadied myself and pressed on. "A body, sewn together with sinew, large and hideous. A patchwork monstrosity. He crafted a machine to harness electricity and gave the creature life. But then he abandoned it.

"The doctor left it to die, but instead it survived with hate in its heart—hate for its creator, hate for all that he held dear," I said. "All because Frankenstein created something he couldn't control and called it monster."

The story pushed past my lips faster and more feverishly than I would've wished, and in my haste I revealed more than I had intended. I swallowed the rest of my wine, and I could feel a swath of warmth growing in my chest. It eased the fear in my ribs, the anger that congealed in the marrow of my bones.

The captain's beard twitched as he frowned. He filled my empty glass before saying, "And this is why you feel you must go North? To seek out this monster?"

I hesitated, then glanced at Ann. "That's all I'll say on it for now," I said.

That only made the captain's frown deepen. He leaned forward, forearms resting upon the table as he searched my face. "And what has any of this got to do with you?"

A question for which I had no easy or honest answer to give him. The truth I would not yet reveal, and still I was reluctant to lie outright. Ann intervened, bless her, giving some blithe, circuitous response about justice and duty. It did nothing to answer the captain's question, but it did seem to distract him enough to move on to other topics. The rest of the evening passed more easily, but I couldn't quite breathe through any of it.

I found myself above deck more often than not in the days that followed, more inclined to feel the biting wind on my cheeks than the inescapable rocking below deck.

Though Ann had little patience for life at sea, I found it refreshingly uncumbersome. Sailors didn't hold to societal norms in quite the same fashion as others, and I found this held true on the *Stirling*. A handful of women even worked on the crew, scientists and deckhands alike. There was a certain freedom to life at sea, and I rather liked the feeling of it.

The seas were rough after leaving port in Havøysund. This last stop in Norway settled us with supplies for the rest of our journey as we pushed further into the Arctic Circle. Though the waters were icy and the skies dark with storms, the true danger was the roiling water. The ocean was unrelenting. It could crash against the hull of the ship until it sank us and still go on raging.

It wasn't raining yet, though the skies were coiled thick and dark overhead. I was huddled in my wool coat on deck, cheeks stinging from the cold as I stared up at the angry sky. Wind snagged curls from my braid and sent them whipping around my ears. Below me, sailors scrambled to secure the crates and barrels of freshly acquired supplies in preparation for the coming storm.

I stood on the second level above the captain's cabin, and between the scurry below and the approaching storm, I somehow went unnoticed.

It was perhaps unwise, but I couldn't bring myself to go below decks just yet. Ann, I knew, was sequestered in our room, likely green from the rocking of the ship and with a little luck too preoccupied to notice my absence.

The ship rolled sharply as a wave crested and fell underneath us. I stumbled and grabbed the railing in front of me. One of the sailors let out a guttural shout of "Gorblimey!" as a row of barrels tumbled overboard—a portion of our ale, if I wasn't mistaken.

A jagged streak of lightning cracked across the sky, illuminating the unsettled seas around us. It began to rain in earnest, some of the drops freezing into rounded icicles against the cold wooden railing. Rain soaked through my coat, the cold settling heavy against me. Lightning flashed again, and an exhilarating tingle of electricity passed across my skin, setting my heart pounding. Waves rose and crashed fifty feet in the air, sending water rushing across the deck as violent gusts of wind whipped against the sails. This was nature at its most formidable, its most deadly.

The ship tilted sharply, and I gripped the railing fiercely as the wind pushed my heavy skirts against my legs. I closed my eyes, breathing in the sharp tang of salty sea air made stronger by the storm. Blood pounded in my ears, an intoxicating feeling of being *alive* passing through me. This was everything Ann had dreaded, and everything I hadn't let myself dare to hope for. There was freedom in this chaos.

One of the sailors noticed me and paused as he was running by. "Miss, it's not safe for you out here. You best get—"

He was interrupted by a shuddering crack that ripped through the air, turning both our heads. A line of rigging had snapped, leaving one of the sails to flap violently in the gusting wind. It pulled dangerously against the mainmast, and it was no small leap to fear that the sail might bring the whole thing down and right through the deck of the ship, leaving us truly foundered.

One of the sailors attempting to secure the rigging was tossed as the sail whipped through the air with all the force of the raging storm behind it. He skidded across the deck, coming to a rest at the port rail. Ignoring the young man beside me, I raced down the companionway and rushed to the fallen sailor's side. I knelt on the water-sloshed deck and turned his neck to search for a pulse.

Unconscious but alive. I breathed a sigh of relief.

The rest of the crew was running about, their shouts and orders drowned out by the noise of the storm. Another sailor, a young woman with trousers banded tight around her waist with a twice-wrapped belt, ran forward. She scurried up the mast, rigging knife between her teeth. Reaching halfway, she began sawing at the rope tethering the loose sail as it continued to lash across the deck. A powerful gust slammed the sail against her, and though she didn't lose her footing, the knife slipped from her grasp and was carried away on the wind. Lost to sea.

I gasped, breath stuttering in my chest. My body reacted on instinct, some ingrained knowledge from my time at sea and a gnawing, bone-deep instinct for survival. I reached down and unsheathed the rigging knife from the leather scabbard of the still-unconscious sailor laid out beside me. My waterlogged skirts hung heavy around my legs, slowing me as I ran toward the mast.

The sailor up in the rigging was already beginning her descent in search of another knife, but I knew there was precious little time. I would meet her halfway.

I started to climb, too scared to look up or down, knife shoved dangerously into the band of my skirt for lack of a better place to hold it. The wood was wet and slick beneath my fingers, iced over in places. My arms burned, unused to this much abuse, and I could only pray they wouldn't give out before I could pass off the knife and climb down again.

Surprise and concern read plain on the sailor's face when she noticed my ascent, but when I shouted "Here!" and dared to pull one hand free to pass up the rigging knife, she leaned down to grab it eagerly.

She clambered back up, but I hesitated where I was, clutching the mast for everything. The spark of hasty courage that had moved me to action began to fade, and only now did I notice the half-frozen pegs slick under my palms and the pull of the swirling storm against my skirts. Unbidden, thoughts of a childhood kite dragged away, twisting and tangled on the wind, rose in my mind. Still, there was no choice but to move.

Skirts weren't meant for climbing, though, and the thick, water-dragged material tangled around my legs as I descended, making it almost impossible for me to maintain my hold. I was two rungs from deck, almost close enough to jump, when the sailor above me finally cut the loose sail free and it came crashing down. I tried to hold tight to the mast, but the sail caught my shoulder and slammed me against the deck.

Long moments (that were likely very short) later, faces swam above me. Rivulets of rain pooled at my eyes, and I tried to blink them away and bring my vision back into focus. People were talking, though it was hopeless for me to discern any words over the noise of the storm and the pounding in my temple. A sturdy arm reached down to help me, and I got to my feet, dizzied from the fall.

A figure rushed toward me through the haze, either of the storm or my vision, I couldn't be sure. She grabbed me round the shoulders, fingers gripping to bruise. "What were you thinking?" Ann shouted over the wind, shaking me for good measure.

My head swam and I must've swayed, because her arms instantly moved to support instead of scold. "You're hurt," she said.

I raised a hand to gingerly feel at my temple, instantly regretting it as even that feather-light touch nearly sent me reeling. "Yes."

"Come on," she said, supporting me around the waist, while someone else (that same sturdy hand from before, perhaps) held on to my other arm. "Let's get you inside."

Once I was settled on the bottom bunk of our room, wrapped in a layer of heavy blankets, that other helping hand revealed itself to be the captain's. He left—somewhat reluctantly—after Ann assured him that though mildly concussed, I would recover with rest.

The continued rocking of the ship and Ann's furious silence did little to calm the pounding in my head as she helped me into dry clothes and settled me back onto the bed. Even the muted scraping as Ann rummaged through the trunk had me clenching my teeth, and I was sure that speaking would kill me, but the silence was worse. I finally said, "You're angry."

"Oh, you've noticed that, have you?" she snapped. Finally finding what she was searching for, she pulled out a blue-tinted bottle of laudanum. "I haven't any honey or sherry, so you'll simply have to take this."

She pulled out the stopper and glared at me expectantly. I felt sure she could find something to sweeten the drug without much trouble, but I understood that this was her way of punishing me. I opened my mouth and allowed her to squeeze a handful of drops onto my tongue. The harsh, bitter sting made me gag, but seeing her expression I dutifully swallowed it down.

She set the bottle aside and then turned back abruptly, her skirt swinging lazily around her legs, still soaked from the storm. "What were you thinking?" she said, not so much asking as demanding.

"I was thinking," I said, struggling to push past the pain in my head, "that if this ship sinks then I'll never find him." I didn't bother to keep the edge of frustration from my voice.

"If this ship sinks, we'll all die, Lilibet," Ann snapped. "Does that matter so little to you?"

"Of course not!" I winced at the sound of my own voice.

"You could've been killed today," Ann said, jabbing a finger in my direction. I tried to point out that I hadn't been, but Ann was not to be dissuaded. She paced the small room, growing increasingly agitated.

"You're going on this, this *crusade*! Endangering us both," Ann said, arms gesticulating sharply. Noticing my pained expression, she calmed a little and came to rest at the edge of the bunk. "Lil, this is a fool's errand. We both heard the news. Frankenstein died on that ship, and his work died with him. Captain Walton's letter—"

"Proves nothing, except that this is where he was headed."

"Call it rumor if you like, but you have no way of knowing that he's out there," said Ann.

"He's there," I said. "I know it."

She reached out a hand to smooth my hair. "You don't know it," she said, and her voice was cracked and heavy with sadness. "You're just desperate for it to be true."

I could feel the laudanum pulling at the edges of my consciousness. Everything was growing fuzzy at the seams.

I shook my head, though it felt like it was lolling outside of my control. "He's there," I insisted, but I could barely hold myself up anymore, and Ann gently pushed against my shoulders, tucking me into bed. She stroked my hand until my breathing deepened and then stood to put the laudanum away.

Perhaps thinking I was asleep or perhaps simply too exhausted to hold it in anymore, Ann let out a shuddering sob. She pressed a hand against her stomach, steadying herself. If I could've dragged myself back into consciousness by force of will, surely I would've done it then to apologize or provide some comfort to her. But my eyelids weighed heavy against my eyes, and I felt myself slipping.

Ann took a steadying breath and smoothed her hair before sitting at the desk to wait out the storm.

That evening and the better part of the next day were spent in a laudanum-induced stupor. I slept, dreamless, and sometimes lay open-eyed in a state somewhere between dreaming and awake. I awoke, finally, rested and feeling mostly well, around sunset.

It didn't take long, however, before things devolved. Ann returned to the room to find me awake if bleary-eyed, but her attention caught on the book at my bedside. She picked up the old, leather-bound journal—to put it away, I expect—and I would've let it pass except I was still somewhat foggy-brained from the medicine.

"No, wait," I said.

She didn't pause to listen, just tied the book shut and, with one hand planted on her hip, said, "These things have brought you nothing but trouble." So we were back to this, the argument we'd picked up and set aside perhaps a dozen times in our years together. These *things*, I knew, were Dr. Frankenstein's old journals, the ones that had set me on this quest in the first place. "They bring out a side of you that spares no thought for your actions, no concern for consequences."

I didn't want to hear it. This argument was well known to me, and I was weary of it. I snatched the journal and clutched it close. "You didn't have to come," I reminded her. "No one forced you, least of all me."

"You gave me no choice once you chose," she said. "You know that." And I did, but I had no intention of admitting it in the moment. Ann was loyal to a fault, and I knew that often—more often than I liked to admit—I asked too much of her, knowing I could.

I rose unsteadily, and Ann reached out in support even in the midst of her ire. She retreated as I moved to place the journal back in the trunk. "I'm sorry that you can't see the importance of this, but I still do."

"There are more important things," she insisted. "The safety of everyone on this ship. Your life."

"That's not—that's never been in question," I said, angered that she would imply otherwise. She raised her eyebrows in disbelief, but I remained determinedly silent, too hurt to reply further.

She swept across the room, arms crossed tight over her chest. "Fine. Shall we talk about the revolver in your trunk?"

I stumbled, just managing to catch myself against the bedpost. The journal tumbled from my hands to fall open-spined against the floor.

I collected the journal, smoothing the crumpled edges. Once I felt more composed, I settled it into the trunk with the other journals, then let the lid of the trunk drop with an unrestrained thud that reverberated between us. "I know perfectly well what I'm doing."

"I see," she said with enough bite to match my tone, though there were still lines of worry across her forehead. "Then you know that you're complicit in whatever comes as a result of the secrets you're keeping. You know you'll be *just as accountable* when this is finished."

"I know my place," I said sharply. "Perhaps it's time you remembered yours. You take too many liberties, Laurie." The words were out of my mouth before I could think to regret them or call them back. I could see the sting of it like a slap across her face, the use of her surname.

Ann straightened, face hardening into an unreadable mask. "Of course, Miss Lavenza."

I faltered, wanting to undo everything I'd said, to snatch my heated words from the air. But it was too late, and each of us had retreated behind cold formality, too hurt and stubborn to do otherwise.

"Excuse me. I need some air," I said, grasping for some way to escape, and I did sound rather breathless, so perhaps it wasn't entirely untrue.

I ran up the companionway, tripping over the hem of my skirt as I sought out the chill of the sea air. I ran until I collided with the starboard railing, tears stinging the corners of my eyes. I shook my head against them, too angry to let them fall.

I wasn't sure who I was angriest with, Ann for pushing us into a fight I'd never wanted, or myself for being so unforgivably cruel.

I'm not sure how long I stood there, staring at the line where the stars met the sea, before the captain found me. He leaned easily against the railing, which only made me stiffen all the more.

He studied me for a long moment before he said, "Your head is better, then?"

Still staring out at the distant sky, I hummed deep in my throat but didn't say anything. I hoped he might leave or at least let us stand in silence. He had things he meant to say, though, and my quiet indifference didn't seem to put him off.

"It took me longer than I'd like to admit to put the pieces together," he said. I glanced over warily at his words, certain this was heading nowhere I would like. He just nodded to himself, looking thoughtful and a little pleased. "Mmm, yes, but I think I've got you figured now, lassie."

I licked my lips, bolstering myself, then turned to face him fully. "And how is that?"

"He's your father." His voice was quiet, almost a whisper, for his own benefit or mine I couldn't discern; if it was for mine, he would've done better to say nothing at all.

"Who?" I asked as though I didn't know.

"The man you spoke of," he said. "This Frankenstein. He was your father."

I tried to ignore him, letting the silence settle around us for so long I wondered if he might just give up and leave. He stayed, however, and at last I let out a harsh, stuttering breath. "Yes," I said.

"You seek to right his wrongs." It wasn't a question.

"Yes."

"Because you see this as your responsibility?"

In the distance, the long spiraled horns of a pod pierced the sea—narwhals, native to these icy waters, breaching and diving in alternating waves. Moonlight glinted off their backs, the twisted tips of their gray horns. Were they seeking better waters? Colder seas?

"My mother is dead because of him," I said, my voice quaking. "He gave life to a creature he couldn't control, called it monster and then abandoned it so that it had no choice but to become one. He unleashed that upon the world. That is my legacy. *That* is the inheritance my father left me."

"And what peace will it bring you, this quest of yours?" he asked.

It struck me as naïve, or narrow-minded maybe, to think that all a girl might want was peace. There might be peace for old men with ordinary names and sea-weathered faces, but what did I know of that? There was fury in my veins; there were shifting continents in my bones. So I told a half truth: "I want only justice," I said.

"What you're doing is no way to find either, lass," he said gently. "Trust an old man who knows. Move on with your life while you still have time."

"I've been searching for two years already, and if I have to search for all the years I'm granted, I will. I will search for as long as I must. And I will get my justice."

"Your justice sounds a lot like revenge to me."

I thought of the revolver hidden away in the bottom of my trunk and the desperate burning in my chest that I felt when I held it. There was a fire kindling in my soul that had been left to simmer for too long. If I was to burn with it, then I would burn.

"I am not a Frankenstein," I said, voice flat and cold. "But I will right my father's wrongs."

I didn't wait for his response, simply spun on the heel of my boot and walked away.

Time stretched and condensed strangely in the days that followed my fight with Ann. I spent much of my time sequestered in the captain's quarters, using the dining table as a desk. McRae didn't seem to mind my presence or the fact that his table was taken over with maps and old letters that I studied obsessively, rechecking theories and making note of locations.

Though I had a number of beautifully modern, hand-painted maps from my uncle's estate, most useful to me was one that had simply fallen from the pages of an old science text in the attic. Sketched on yellowing parchment, it bore no legend, no bar scale to delineate measures; all that spoke to its accuracy and purpose was a scrawled signature at the bottom right, a barely legible VF.

If my father's search for the creature led him on this route to the Arctic, as his maps and Walton's letter suggested, then surely I was on the right track. Surely little else mattered.

I returned to my room long into the night, when I could be certain Ann was already strewn across the top bunk asleep or else pretending to be.

She was gone in the mornings before I woke. We passed one another in this way, rarely acknowledging each other except in fractured greetings that left me feeling cracked open and cold.

"Excuse me, Miss Lavenza, I was just leaving."

"That's quite all right, I—"

But she would be gone before I could say more, though even if she had lingered I could think of little to say that might undo the damage I'd done.

I was under no illusion about who was at fault for this fracture in our relationship. From my earliest memories, I'd always had a knack for pushing away the people I loved. My father who never saw me as a reason to stay, my uncle who too soon tired of my presence. Even my mother died. And Ann, oh, I knew Ann was slow to anger, but she was even slower to forgive.

So I turned to the only thing left to me, the reason we'd come on this forsaken ship in the first place: my quest to right the sins of my father. I buried myself in books; I read and reread Robert Walton's letters; I traced the lines of longitude and latitude across maps until my eyes burned; I studied firsthand accounts I'd collected over the years, jotting down an ink-smudged list of every possible location.

I felt sure if I just looked hard enough, searched long enough, some line of text or scribbled landmark would reveal itself and guide me toward my goal.

Meals passed me by unnoticed. Sleep became a torturous affair. Rather than medicating, I returned to my room later and later each day. Childhood memories of my father, distant and laudanum-hazed as he exorcised his own demons, weighed too heavy on my mind to allow for anything else. We drew closer to the Arctic, but I was feeling increasingly detached from everything, including myself.

"No more," McRae said late one afternoon.

"Excuse me?"

"No more of this sulking or obsession or what have you," he said, slapping an open-palmed hand against the maps I had scattered across the desk.

"I—I'm sure I don't know what you—"

He interrupted without a thought for common courtesy. "Aye, you do," he said. "You're acting like a bairn, and I'll have no more of it. You'll speak to that companion of yours if I have to lock the both of you in this room to do it."

I pressed the heels of my hands against my eyes. I was so tired. "I don't—I don't believe she much wants to speak to me at the moment."

That I had tried more than once to do so went unsaid. My guilt and shame were more than sufficient without him knowing the whole of it.

"She's your friend, aye?" he asked, some of the harshness gone from his voice as I finally looked up at him.

"My only friend," I admitted with a sad smile. Ann, who had never abandoned me. Ann, who endured danger and seasickness to be by my side. She would run herself ragged to make my life easier.

"Well, then," he said, clapping his hands in conclusion. "That settles the matter, mmh?"

"Settles what, exactly?" I said, wary of the answer and equally sure that I already knew what it would be.

"If you're truly friends, you owe it to each other to make things right."

"I don't think it's that simple," I said. Some hurts couldn't be soothed with words. Some people didn't deserve forgiveness.

"Never is, lass," the captain told me. He went to the door but paused with his hand on the handle. "You'll lose yourself in this if you continue on alone," he said. "She grounded you. You've come untethered without her."

He left, and my body sank down against the desk. The exhaustion in my bones seeped into my words. "I know," I said, even though the captain was gone and there was no one left to hear.

We made landfall that night, though icefall might have been a truer description. I was up late, passing the hours in the hold below deck reserved for the sled dogs. They were more wolf than dog, and certainly not good companionship, but they were held in kennels, and it was the steady undercurrent of their breathing more than anything that drew me to them. The map signed with my father's initials and spread across my lap was my true focus still.

The ship shuddered and creaked, telltale signs that it was pushing through ice, and I rose quickly to look out the porthole. Ice crumpled around the hull, then smoothed out into a calm, rolling expanse beyond it. Glacial mountains in the distance created a looping hook that dropped into a deep, parabolic valley. A strangely familiar outline, considering I had never yet made it this far north.

And then my weary mind made the connection. I clutched the map to my chest, crushing the fragile paper in my fist, then frantically smoothed it next to the porthole until the lines of the horizon lined up with the sketch on the back of the map. The sketch that showed a valley, circled in harsh lines of charcoal, beside a hooked peak.

What I had taken for a half-finished drawing before, I now understood to be a landmark—a landmark my father had used to mark a base, perhaps.

I raced from the hold, ignoring the dogs' disgruntled yaps. I knew what needed to be done. My mind had been made up before my conversation with the captain, before boarding the *Stirling*, even. And now I finally saw my way.

It was early morning, long before Ann would wake and while the rest of the ship was still asleep. I snuck into the room, careful of the creaking floorboards, and opened my trunk. I pushed aside voluminous skirts and neatly folded shirts until my fingers met cold metal. My hand curled around the handle and pulled out a pinfire revolver, silver and heavily engraved. The first purchase I ever made for myself.

The metal was cool and comforting in my hand. I hefted it, reacquainting myself with its weight, the feel of it in my grip. I pulled a brass cartridge out of the small munitions box. Lining the pin of the cartridge up with the groove in the back of the revolver, I quietly clicked it into place. Carefully, I placed the revolver deep in the left pocket of my skirt. I closed the trunk and slipped out of the room.

There was only one sailor on watch as I spirited my way across deck toward the lifeboats, and, as he was asleep in the crow's nest, little stealth was required. Lowering the boat without assistance was a somewhat trickier affair, but I had seen it done enough times to manage. Then, silent and unwavering, it was only a matter of making my way across the ice.

The ship had moved deeper into the ice floe overnight, and I made slow progress across the treacherous terrain until it thickened into solid ground, the mountains looming in the distance. Between them was the valley my father had marked on his map.

Today I would find justice—one way or another.

Even bundled as I was in layer upon layer of fabric, mittened and capped under a heavy wool coat, the Arctic chill seeped through. It burrowed deep, taking root under my skin as I made my way across the white landscape. Everything was hazy and bright in the early hours of morning.

In hindsight, I see how foolhardy, how arrogant I was to take to the ice alone with nothing but the hope of a hand-drawn map and a gun loaded with a single bullet. I had taken no supplies, no tent or matches or hardtack to safeguard my life against the dangers of this place. My only thought was of my quest, and I was single-minded to a fault in pursuit of it.

I don't know how long I wandered, hours or days. The sun rarely sets in an Arctic spring. The cold was fierce, and heavy flakes of snow began to fall, and the likelihood of my survival seemed to diminish with every passing second on the ice. Predators and frostbite and starvation—the dangers were untold, and I was woefully unprepared.

The snow thickened until I could no longer make out my own mittened hand held out against the wind in front of me. The mountains had long since disappeared behind a snowy haze. Was I even going in the right direction? It was impossible to say.

In the end, it was he who found me.

Across the way, I saw him, vague and looming, as in a dream. His frame was deformed by a bundle of jackets much like mine. He called out, with a wave of his arm, urging me toward him. Behind him, I could just make out the outline of a shack with a tail of curling smoke. I had reached the valley.

He called again, waving me to safety, but I stood frozen. I was too far out, still, to distinguish any features, but who else could it be? Who else but the two of us might be found here on the ice?

I pressed my palm against the outline of the revolver through my skirt, feeling the comforting weight of it against my thigh, and slowly approached.

I was almost upon him before he seemed to recognize me, eyes widening, in first surprise and then something like horror. Or, perhaps it was joy. His features were a familiar mystery to me, grown craggy with age. His eyes, though half shut against the glinting ice, were the same. I shuddered to see something of myself in them.

"Elizabeth?" he asked, voice shaking. He stumbled forward, as if compelled by some unseen force to come to me. "Elizabeth."

Hearing the name of my mother from his lips sent a shiver of fury down my spine. "That is not my name!" I shouted.

He sighed, the rejection draining all expectations from him. "Daughter," he began instead, and though I liked it even less, I let him continue, "you should not be here."

"You haven't given me much choice," I told him.

"I left to protect you," he began.

"Protect me!" I scoffed, and there was no hope of hiding from the emotion in my voice. I could feel it burning a fire up my throat and through my wind-chilled veins. "You abandoned us. My mother is dead because of you!"

"That creature—"

"Don't," I said. "Don't you dare place the blame on that creature when you're the one who made it what it was."

"Elizabeth, please. At least, let me bring you inside . . ."

"My name is Lilibet." I bit out the words, teeth snapping against my tongue.

He didn't reply, though his mouth twisted. His face was lined and worn tired by the years. I could recognize the broad strokes of the features, but the man himself was a mystery, broken down by time and guilt.

"I tried to make it right, child," he said, finally, after long moments had hung suspended over the ice. "I did what I could."

"*What you could*?" I clenched my jaw against the fury working at my throat. "You did nothing. You let that creature run free! You could've *stayed*; you could've taught it how to be or at least taken care of it after you failed to teach it anything at all! You could've taken responsibility for all the lives you cost us. Anything . . . you could've done anything but what you did."

I hoped to hurt him, to break him open so he could bleed like I did. I could feel the shape of the revolver in my hand, still hidden inside my skirts, finger looped around the trigger.

"I'm sorry," he said. "I'm sorry I didn't do more then, but I brought the creature to justice." His voice broke when he added, "For your mother. For you."

I offered no acceptance, no forgiveness, but still a shadow passed from his face. He seemed, suddenly, ten years younger, still too old for his true age but somehow less burdened. There was a hope there, maybe for whatever it was he thought I was here to do.

"I brought you justice," he said quietly, almost to himself.

"And now I'm here to bring you yours." I drew the revolver from my pocket, slowly raising it level to his chest. My thumb pulled the hammer so that with one easy press of my index finger, it would release, smashing into the cartridge and igniting the powder inside.

He didn't tremble under my aim. It occurred to me that he didn't know me very well, might not believe me capable of doing such a thing as this. But he was staring into my eyes—hazel like my mother's but hardened with fury—and I knew he understood.

My aim didn't waver, but the weight of the revolver, only waiting for me to press my finger against the trigger, was pulling at the muscles of my arm. The snowfall was beginning to lighten, and beams of light glinted off the icy peaks. He watched me, face calm and gentle in a way I had never before seen. "It's all right."

My arm shook, and I could hear them approaching—Ann, McRae, and the others. Ann had woken to an empty room, and she must've known. I hefted the revolver in my hand, reaffirming my aim at the heart of the man who had taken so much from me, from so many.

From the corner of my eye, I could see Ann running toward me with half a dozen men and a team of sled dogs behind her. I could guess at the unfiltered mix of emotions playing across her face—anger and fear and desperation—though my gaze never wavered from my aim. Just before Ann reached me, the captain grabbed her and held her back.

"Don't do this, Lilibet, *please*," Ann begged. I took comfort in hearing my name from her and hoped it meant she had forgiven me—hoped it meant she could still find it in herself to forgive me for whatever was to come.

"You don't need to do this, Miss Lavenza," said Captain McRae. I could sense them all at the edge of my vision, treading carefully across the ice as if I were an animal they feared might attack. "There are other ways."

Tears froze against my lashes, hateful and unwanted. There were no other ways. There were no other choices.

He stumbled forward suddenly, the man I aimed to kill. The sounds of shouting and guns being drawn surrounded me as Frankenstein pushed toward me until the barrel of my revolver was pressed into his chest.

"Do it," he hissed, voice cracked and desperate. Snow and drops of ice were frozen in his beard. I shook my head mutely, feeling as if I'd taken a wrong turn somewhere half a continent back. It wasn't meant to be like this. Still, my finger didn't release from the trigger.

"*Lilibet, please!*" Ann shouted.

I stared into my father's eyes, and my finger tightened at the trigger. I lowered the gun. My chin trembled, and I choked back a sob, feeling as if I was stepping away from the edge of a cliff.

Doubled over, breath snatched from my lungs, I turned my gaze back to my father. "You will return with me to Ingolstadt," I said, feeling several hundred years older than my twenty-some years. "You will face trial for the sins you've committed in the name of science and God."

My father scrambled at me, to attack or pry the revolver from my hands and end this himself—I'm not sure, but McRae and the crew restrained him. I was knock-kneed, frozen to the bone, by the time the sailors had my father in hand, and Ann had gingerly—like I was a wild creature she hoped not to spook—taken the revolver from my hand.

Her mittened grip was firm on my shoulder, grounding me in this frozen wasteland. McRae's eyes met mine as I straightened. "I assumed you were after the monster," he said to me.

I said nothing. I was weary and wary, all too aware that I had been less than a thought away from committing murder in front of my closest friend and a handful of near strangers.

Ann wrapped an arm around my shoulder, and I sank into her embrace, letting her guide me back across the ice shelf.

They kept my father in a locked room on the side of the ship opposite mine—though who exactly this was meant to protect was unclear. We were returning to the continent, where his fate would be left for others to decide, and in the meantime there was little to do but wait with simmering thoughts. And simmering guilt.

Chief among those guilts was my fight with Ann. Though we were speaking again, there was a chill to our relationship where before there was none. We settled into an uncertain normalcy that I found unbearable, so after several long days of this—and knowing the center would not hold—I gathered my skirts and my courage and returned to our room.

Ann was seated on the small wooden chair next to the bunks, pulling viciously at a line of thread on the shirt she was mending. She glanced up as I entered but otherwise ignored me in favor of the shirt in her lap. I sat on the bed, smoothing out my skirts nervously, studying the lines of consternation on her face and wondering how many of them were there for the mending and how many for me.

The thread snapped at a particularly violent tug, and she clicked her tongue angrily before tossing away the ruined thread and holding the needle up to her eye to begin again. Moments of watching her mangle the strand as she tried to thread the needle left me agitated.

"Let me have it," I said, impatiently, holding out my hand for the blouse. Ann sighed, and I snatched the cloth and needle from her before she could do any further damage. Pushing my skirts out of the way, I sat heavily on the bed, inspecting her handiwork now lying in my lap. "Honestly, how you became a lady's maid with less skill at the needle than a child . . ."

"I can sew," she said tersely.

"Just not buttons, then?" I said, looking up at her to smile just a little.

She huffed as I turned my attention back to the shirt, pulling loose the tangled threads Ann had left and taking up the needle to begin again. I chewed the edge of my lip, waiting for her reply. And then it came. "You can't just come in here and pretend as though everything's fine," she said.

I paused midstitch, needle hovering over the shirt. "I'm not," I said softly.

"Of course you are," she said. "It's what you always do."

The hurt and frustration in her voice were evident. I began sewing again, threading the needle through the small holes of the button in the hope that it would provide enough distraction to keep me level-headed. "I'm not, Ann."

"Oh, no?"

"No, I—I came to apologize," I said, looking up from my stitching. Her mouth hung open in surprise. She hadn't expected that. The realization that she hadn't thought me capable of an apology sent a lancing pain through my chest, to know that she could think so little of me, to know that I'd perhaps given her reason to.

"I *am* apologizing." I set the mending aside and looked to her, waiting until she looked back at me. "I'm sorry."

"For which part exactly?" she asked, and I probably deserved that and more.

"All of it. But especially, especially for what I said before. You're my friend, and I treated you as if that didn't mean anything to me. It does. And I'm—I'm sorry if I've ever made you feel otherwise."

I brushed angrily at a telltale burning in the corners of my eyes. Gently, she took my hand.

"I forgive you," she said. "If only because you've run yourself entirely ragged, and I feel sure you'll concoct some other harebrained scheme and get yourself killed if I don't." She squeezed my hand, and the corners of her lips turned up in an encouraging expression. I winced through a smile.

"I don't deserve you," I said.

"Almost certainly." But she said it with a wry smile. "And now? You found your father. What will you do next?"

That was the question. What was left, after all was said and done? "Now I have one more thing to see to," I said.

She knew my revolver had been taken away and hidden from me at least until we reached dry land, and maybe longer. Still, she looked worried. I couldn't find it in me to assure her of my sanity or my intention to see my father face trial. Somehow I doubted she would believe me even if I'd tried. Instead I squeezed her hand one last time and left her with what I hoped was a reassuring look.

Across the ship, a sailor stood watch in front of a door at the far corner of a hall. I recognized her as the same woman who had cut loose the sail during the storm. She seemed reluctant to let me in but eventually relented, perhaps feeling indebted to me for my help on that day some weeks ago. I was given five minutes.

He was hunched on the edge of his cot, thin and ragged. He looked smaller than he had out on the ice shelf, drawn in on himself, and maybe it was the small room—so narrow his knees almost touched the wall opposite his bed—or maybe it was just me truly seeing him for the first time.

"Have you come to finish it?" he asked me. I thought I saw a hopeful glint in his eye.

I hesitated then shook my head. I wasn't sure what I had come for, but I hadn't come for that.

He shrank back, something dimming almost imperceptibly behind his eyes. "I'm tired," he told me. "There is no peace left for me in this life."

My fury almost sparked at that, but I smothered it. I focused on the weary curve of his body instead. He was small and weak and defenseless here. It was easy to hate the idea of him. Facing the all-too-human reality in front of me, however, inspired something more like pity.

"Maybe we don't deserve peace," I said softly.

"We?" he said. His head tilted. "What monsters have you created lately?"

I shook my head mutely, unsure of what to say. There was a darkness in his eyes that I recognized in my soul. I wanted nothing more than to give in to it—and nearly had—but I knew coming back from it would be impossible. The shrinking man in front of me was evidence enough of that.

I turned to go. Whatever I hoped to find here, I couldn't find it with him—not now and perhaps not ever. If the man I knew—the one I remembered in some distant, childish way as "father"—was still in there, I couldn't find him.

He spoke as I reached for the door: "The monster knew he was a monster," he said. Then, quietly, "What does that make us?"

I left without another word. I had no answers for him and even less sympathy. He was old and sick with guilt, and I hated him for it. I hated him for making me hate him, but I hated him more for the way he made me hate myself.

My name is Lilibet Lavenza, and I spent many years on a quest for a monster who turned out to be only a man.

I have no moral, no great lesson here for you to learn, but please know this: I am my own, above all else. The mistakes I made—though in my father's footsteps—were mine. The choices I pushed on myself and others fall only to me.

I belong terribly, awfully, to myself.

RACHEL BRITTAIN is an alumna of Vanderbilt University but currently lives and writes in Arkansas. Her short film, *The Delivery Girl*, has been screened at film festivals in Los Angeles and New York, and her novelette, "End of the World Talk Show," can be found in *Hyperion and Theia, Vol. One: Saturnalia* (Radiant Crown Publishing, 2017).

13

A True History of the Notorious Mr. Edward Hyde

Tony Eprile

'YDE'S THE NAME. EDWARD 'YDE . . . OR HYDE, AS EDUCATED FOLK
like yourself would have it. That's my real name, although for the past
fifty years, Hyde has stayed hidden under the moniker of Edward Layman. To the good people here in the West Midlands, I'm just Layman or
Ed, no different from nobody else, a stand-up bloke, a hard worker, but
no boss's tool, fond of his pint of bitter and mild and always ready for a
joke or sing-along. Only my cousin Vic—and now you—knows my real
name, the one that sends chills up the world's spine. As Hyde, I've been
called a deformed and depraved creature of hell, a vicious human jugger-
naut. "Edward Hyde, alone in the ranks of mankind, was pure evil." Nice
words, I must say. Courtesy of none other than the ultimate toffee nose,
Dr. Jekyll, Harley Street specialist and man noted for his good works.
Where's the charity in such talk? I ask. And yet, because he went to the

right schools and said things in such a reasonable, sophisticated way, you believe him. Funny how people can be educated but not smart, i'n' it?

Jekyll. Even today I can't hear his name without the hair on my neck rising in pure animal rage. And to think I used to admire the man. I wanted to be like him, to talk posh and live in a house filled with elegant appurtenances instead of mere furniture. Even when it finally penetrated the great Roman wall of my thick prole's head that I was hopelessly trapped in Dr. Jekyll's rotten web (while he grew bloated and fat on my helpless struggles), I still wanted what he had. You see, Jekyll—let him rot in hell, appurtenances and all—had class. And that, as Cousin Vic would say, is what it's all about.

I was just recently turned twenty when I met the illustrious Dr. Jekyll, and of all the days in my life, that one stands out clearest in memory. There was a spring-sharp brightness, sunlight pouring in like newly minted sovereigns. Not at all the usual pewter-gray skies of London, and I was cocksure and full of myself that day. My luck was up, or so I thought. There's something about being young that makes you feel undefeatable; I had a nice chunk of money weighing down my pockets and raw pleasure in the unfettered, wiry roll of my youthful muscles as I strolled the streets of London. The evening before, I had landed an unexpected five guineas. I'd gone with some of my mates to one of Jimmy Wilshire's fighting cellars. This was not one of your Marquess of Queensbury bouts of fisticuffs but the aptly called "Big Knuckle"—where it's bare knuckles and bare feet and you fight on until you or your opponent are knocked senseless. It was strictly out of the bounds of The Law, of course, but any night of the week, if you knew where to look, you could find yourself in a small, ill-lit room in which two brawny boyos were laying into each other on the roped-off mats in the center to the cheers of a crowd of red-faced men yelling themselves hoarse. And it wasn't just commoners who frequented Jimmy Wilshire's cellars but toffs putting down pound bets on their favorites and standing close enough to the action to get blood on their evening jackets or to catch the occasional flying molar for a souvenir.

Hard Anthony had just knocked his opponent cold in mere minutes of combat, and the barker was now offering a purse of five guineas to anyone in the audience game enough to spend ten minutes in the ring with him. I had been an occasional stevedore on the London docks and had taken part in my share of pub brawls, where the stake was your own skin and the weapons included knives, if you had one, and anything else that came to hand if you did not. So, with my friends' raucous encouragement, I took on the bet. Hard Anthony came up to me with a friendly grin and a hand extended for a gentlemanly shake. I'd been caught by just such a bit of commonplace treachery in one of the few street tussles I'd lost, so I pretended to let myself be pulled off-balance but quickly ducked under the flying fist that was following up fast behind the handshake. It was Hard Anthony's turn to be off guard, and I took the wind out of his sails with a lightning-quick knee to the groin, the good old Ringsend uppercut. He was knackered good and proper, and though he was a tough berk, practiced in a range of dirty tricks—like greasing himself all over with oil so you couldn't get a purchase—I'm no sluggard when it comes to a barney, and it didn't take all that long before I tossed his unconscious carcass into a pile of chairs that seemed to have been placed there for just that purpose. My only injuries were a few scratches—Hard Anthony clawed like a woman—and a bruise under my eye from a vicious head butt.

That is how on a bright morning, with my head still cottony from the rounds of Jimmy Wilshire's home-brewed gin and porter that I had treated and been treated to, I happened to be walking along Harley Street and paused for a moment next to a brass shingle announcing the name Henry Jekyll, MD, DCL, LLD, FRS, and enough other initials to show that the inhabitant could split himself in half and open two medical practices. It recalled to me a condition that was a cause of some embarrassment, the results of a few moments of friendliness with a comely scullery maid. Just thinking about it brought on the discomfort, a burning exaggerated by the quantity of liquor I had consumed the night before. Jingling the still half-full purse in my trouser pocket, I clambered up the stairs and pounded the fateful knocker.

I found myself quite humbled by my surroundings: grim Poole the manservant in his somber duds, the unobtrusively expensive furnishings, and the resounding church-like quiet of the high-ceilinged chambers. Jekyll, a tall man with wispy hair combed back from his forehead, was equally imposing in his fine-tailored clothing, but he knew what he was about and had me quickly stripped and diagnosed . . . a salve administered and injunctions to use more salve at regular intervals and to drink large quantities of water, only water. "For the next two weeks, you will just have to be satisfied with the fact that the City of London rocks gently upon an artesian well and not a brewery," he said with mocking seriousness. "And, of course, abstinence of another kind for the same period is a definite must."

All this was something I could easily live with, and I was relieved to have taken care of the problem so handily. A quite different shock was in store for me. The bill Jekyll presented me with was for five guineas. I now eyed the gracious furniture with bitterness, having seen how it came to be purchased. This was more than I earned in two weeks of stevedoring and, unfortunately, more than remained to me in the little purse that I now emptied onto the tabletop. Three pounds six was all that was left after the previous night's generosity.

"That's all I've got, governor. And for me that's a tidy sum of money."

"I've no doubt. But I'm not so sure the police would see it in that light." Jekyll looked at me thoughtfully, murmuring to himself: "A fine example of the unconscious brute side of human nature. Enters here without a thought to payment and consequences . . . a certain animal magnetism . . . the beast happy in its ignorant cavern . . ."

He grew contemplative, studying me for a while. Then he began to question me closely as to how I had come about the bruise under my eye and other particulars. When I balked at telling him at length of the source of my little illness, he gazed at me coldly and offered to dispatch Poole to seek out the nearest policeman. But when I told him the details of my rendezvous with the scullion in the small alcove behind the coal shuttle of her employers' house, his friendliness returned, and he smiled delightedly while he drank in the details like an old sea dog confronted with his first pint of shoretime ale.

"Marvelous," he said, examining his own plump, manicured hand with manifest satisfaction. "It's an ill wind that brings no good, Mr. Hyde. I think we can come to an arrangement that will be of benefit to both of us.

"You see before you," he continued, "a man who is known and respected throughout all London—a doer of good deeds, a pillar of society. My stature, nay, my very upbringing—the air I breathe in these luxurious chambers—constrains me to act always in a civilized manner. Not for me the brute spontaneity of a quick dalliance behind the coal scuttle, the thump on the head for the fool who dares look at me cross-eyed. No, I must comport myself with decency at all times, fettered by my higher place in the scale of evolution as surely as the gallows thief is prevented from fleeing to freedom by his leg irons."

Jekyll continued in this manner for some time. I did not understand all of what he was saying at that instant, but I gathered that I was to be his proxy. My work was to indulge in my animal lusts, and all I had to do was report my doings to Dr. Jekyll in order to be forgiven my debt and receive a handsome retainer besides.

"Go forth and be wicked, Hyde," Jekyll intoned as he let me out the back door of his building, the entrance I was to use from now on in any communication with him.

At first, I thought that Dr. Jekyll was either cracked or just plain having me on, but the following Friday—the date he had set for our next encounter—curiosity took my feet down the back lane on the far side of Harley Street. On my way there, an odd incident occurred. A small girl dressed in a striped pinafore was so intent on chasing a child's hoop, which she kept balanced by tapping it with a light cane, that she ran full tilt into me. I lifted her up, helped her retrieve the hoop, and gave her a halfpenny to bring back the smile to her limpid, innocent face.

Approaching the cellar door, I rapped once on its thick oak paneling, thinking that if there was no response, I could chalk the whole thing off to a moment's eccentricity on the doctor's part. To my surprise, the door swung open immediately, and Jekyll ushered me inside with every sign of having been eagerly awaiting my arrival.

"So, my good Hyde, what acts of gross turpitude have you committed since last we met?" he demanded.

Since I had been obeying his orders to stay clear of intoxicating beverages, my time had passed slowly and with little opportunity for mischief. Racking my brains, I thought of a little trick I had played some months before on a certain fishmonger in the Haymarket. The man was a fussy sort, always checking the balance of his weighing scales to make quite sure some poor old missus wasn't getting away with a free sliver of fin or tail. While my best buddy, Townsend, distracted the man—"What's this, then? A grouper? Never heard of it. Got any eels? I could go for a nice eel"—I quickly nicked a couple of the weights that served to balance out the scale in graded half ounces. Pretending it had happened just days before, I narrated this history, much to Dr. Jekyll's delight.

"Capital, Hyde, capital. A little rough justice, if you will. And what else? What other means has Satan found to tempt you?"

I was forced to plunder my memory's storehouse—surely I had not done only good deeds in the interval?—when, suddenly, inspiration struck. I told Jekyll the story of the child and her hoop . . . only, this time there was no stopping to help her up and dust her off. Instead, I joyously trod the helpless infant into the ground with my heavy work boots, indifferent to her terrified screams. Jekyll shivered as I described how the little hoop cracked underfoot like a chicken bone.

"And you didn't look back at all, Hyde?" he asked, rubbing his hands with glee.

"Not even once, Dr. Jekyll. Not once."

Jekyll gave me ten pounds and said he looked forward to our meeting the following week. As I was leaving, he called me back. "It's almost noon now. If you walk towards Cavendish Square, you'll be sure to encounter a stout gentleman dressed in a finely tailored charcoal-gray overcoat complete with beaver-skin top hat. In all likelihood, he'll have in his hands an ebony cane that is the very twin of this one. The man's name is Utterson, and he has an appointment with me. Spatter some mud on him for me— hey, Hyde? Or, better yet, smear some chalk on the back of his overcoat."

For all his sophistication, Dr. Jekyll's notion of evildoing was still that of a schoolboy.

For about six months, the arrangement between Jekyll and myself was useful for us both. For Jekyll, it was a chance to experience vicariously a way of being at complete odds with his habitual one. For me, it was a steady source of good money . . . but more than that, it was an opportunity to live outside the limits of my ilk and income. I valued the time spent with Jekyll, and I even borrowed some of his books to go through afterwards in my own time. Jekyll had a command of the Queen's English that I frankly envied, and I would find myself assuming some of his mannerisms and using some of his more eloquent locutions. See?—"locutions," that's a Jekyll word. His influence is with me even now.

Of course, there were difficulties. One day, I wore to our cellar meeting a fancy singlet modeled on Jekyll's own that I had bought with some of the money I had saved up. When he saw me in it, far from being flattered, he was furious.

"I pay you because you bring me the stink of the gutter, Hyde, not the scent of Savile Row," he railed. "Don't try to turn yourself into a gentleman, my boy. It would be a ridiculous sight: like a bullock laying eggs!"

He softened a little under my injured glare. "Come now, don't look at me like that. I suppose we all have a right to play at being what we're not—I, to be a brute, and you, to be a fine gentleman—but we need to keep some perspective, not let it go to our heads."

I suppose if that had been the only problem, I could have borne with it without too much complaint. What did it matter if Jekyll mocked my lack of education, and even more so my desire to make up for it? Let him be superior and condescending. It didn't stop me from learning what I wanted to learn. As Vic says about me, I can talk management, and I can talk mates.

No, the real problem was a certain universal fact of human nature: yesterday's vice is worth about as much as yesterday's daily paper. The wine of my evil deeds soon stopped intoxicating Jekyll; he must have stronger stuff! From being content to hear about my misdeeds, he went to being an observer . . . then observer became participant, and the downfall of us both was assured.

It started off with Jekyll having me stage a bare-fist bout in his capacious cellar. The audience was "a select few" of Jekyll's friends, men whom he trusted, classmates and old boys from Jekyll's public school. Among them was Utterson, who chose not to recognize in me the churl who had befouled his greatcoat with a hearty slap on the back. Another was a spry, white-haired gentleman named Sir Danvers Carew, an MP and a peer of the realm, no less. We put on a good show for the fine gentlemen. Too good a show, in fact, for I got carried away one day and beat my opponent, a young ruffian I'd known from the docks, into an insensate pulp.

You see, as Jekyll became more depraved in his desires, so I became more corrupt. I came to revel in the role into which he had cast me, like a music hall performer who forgets that it's all a mickey-take. With the money Jekyll gave me, I found I could buy the downtrodden, attractive youth of London. There was not a young household maid or messenger lad that I could not entice into Jekyll's cellar, where the practice of vice had achieved a rare pitch of refinement. These are memories I prefer not to call to mind, the times I spent swaggering around the city bullying my peers with my own physical strength and Jekyll's pecuniary wherewithal. My encounters with women ceased to be a jolly lark, a moment's warm reprieve from the cares of daily life. Instead, they were a transaction.

Things began to heat up for me, dangers that were the result of my new life. Jimmy Wilshire was out to get me for intruding on his territory, or so it was rumored. Hard Anthony himself was supposed to be waiting for me in some dark lane or courtyard, armed with cosh and shiv. At first I didn't care. I borrowed Jekyll's tough ebony cane and let it be known on the street that Hard Anthony had better stay out of my way. But there were other things that did begin to bother me: The way my former mates avoided me or only sought me out when the need for lucre grew overpowering. The hard-edged way the girls now looked at me . . . how they let me debauch them with my five- and ten-pound notes. People had become afraid of me. The drubbing I'd given to my youthful sparring partner (it had cost me a tidy sum to mollify him while he recovered from his injuries) had become part of city lore and was much exaggerated in the telling. Even Townsend, the jokester who had grown up just two houses away from me and who as long as I knew him was always up for a lark . . . he only came to me when he needed money, acted sullen and fearful, let me push him around without answering back. I was coming to know Jekyll's loneliness, the knowledge that no one gives a hoot for you yourself but only for the bit of silver that might fall their way. Not to say I didn't take pride in my newfound power—in the very independence Jekyll's money bought me—but it was slowly, much too slowly, beginning to sink in that all this was playacting. I had given up my own soul to become another man's thrall.

I will not bore you, dear reader, with a lengthy account of my downward spiral in the ensuing months. Jekyll himself berated me for "opening the gates of hell" to him, while simultaneously charging me with the arrangement of ever more wanton acts of dissipation. One moment he would threaten to bring in the Law on the grounds that I was extorting money from him; the next moment he would beg me not to disrupt his only true moments of pleasure. Many times I thought of simply disappearing, of leaving without a word, but always the lure of Jekyll's fascinating character—along with the sense of invincibility brought on by a steady supply of cash and the protecting shield of the doctor's reputation—brought me back. The truth is that I, too, was addicted to the heady fumes of unbridled wickedness, the gratifying crunch of cartilage beneath knuckle, the wild debauches in the cellar. And yet I was racked by the twin goads of conscience and fear. As Jekyll one day said, we were "like man's twin demons of good and evil locked in mortal embrace while our worldly bark teeters on the edge of the waterfall."

Late one night, as all things must, the whole charade came to an end. It was one of those dark, brooding nights when all but the friendless are home in a warm bed beside the pale embers of a dying fire. Patches of mist floated hither and yon like untethered wraiths, and I wandered alone like them, lost in embittered reflection. All of a sudden, a slender, white-haired figure appeared in front of me. It was Sir Danvers Carew, who seemed both surprised and delighted to see me. Carew was a quiet sort, with the distinguished air of a man who knows his own importance. He kept himself aloof during our mad carousals, but he was always there to the last minute, smiling to himself, sitting a little to one side.

"Ah, it's Henry Jekyll's hired bravo," Carew remarked in his melodious voice and began to inquire earnestly and sympathetically after my health. In the next moment, he made a proposal to me of such audacious indecency that my mind reeled. Suddenly, the Spirit of Justice, of right and wrong, that had been until now bottled up inside me as in a pressure boiler, rose up with irresistible force. With a shout, I sprang upon Carew and knocked him to the ground, where I dealt out my answer to his disgusting suggestion with Jekyll's ebony cane. A moment later I came to my senses, and tossing the shattered cudgel aside, I fled.

I wandered away from the city on foot, my mind cast loose from its moorings. For several days I walked, stopping only occasionally to rest or buy some food, and eventually I found myself in the West Midlands, the industrial heart of our fabled isle. It was late afternoon, but it might as well have been night, the way the clouds of factory smoke blotted out the pallid sun. The clang of machinery was almost deafening, and here and there flames shot out to silhouette a human figure as a boiler door was opened to feed the mechanical beast. The place uncannily resembled an oil painting of hell that had hung in Jekyll's office, but for me it was an honest spot, one where I could preserve my anonymity in the midst of other rough, working folks like myself. I remembered that a favorite cousin lived here, Vic Goodston, and by dint of asking in various local pubs, I was soon able to locate him. Vic helped me get a job at a local foundry, where the softened pads of my fingers and palms soon acquired the calluses of forthright toil. It was work that brought me back to myself. No thought was required, none of the fancy words I had learned while hanging about with the upper crust . . . just a steady hand and muscles that could endure a full day of shoveling coal into a giant, blasting furnace.

As my mind healed itself, the fear that I would be discovered and hauled off to the gallows became ever stronger. Vic's discrete inquiries helped allay my fears as we gradually pieced together the story of why

Scotland Yard was no longer searching for the violent madman and killer, Edward Hyde. The first shock was that Dr. Henry Jekyll himself was dead, and by his own hand. Before downing the deadly draught of prussic acid, he had written out a lengthy manuscript, detailing the fiction you all know so well.

Don't believe for a moment that Jekyll was motivated by any desire to aid the man he had so grievously injured. No, Jekyll was simply being true to his race—avoiding the scandal that would bring down not only himself but his friend Utterson and the rest of the select crowd who frequented Jekyll's cellar. The world could not be allowed to think that its most elite denizens harbored tastes that can charitably be called unsavory. No, far better if society should think that by taking a few salt compounds, the noble Jekyll was turned into a beast, a mere day laborer, a stinking, odious hand-for-hire controlled not by his brain but his brute instincts. It was a fabrication that would not have taken in a child, but the bonded word of aristocrats like Utterson and of the police detectives, whose nests were feathered by a limitless supply of pound notes, was enough to convince a gullible public. I suppose I should be grateful to Jekyll for providing me with a way out, a substantial grant on my lease in this vale of tears, but I'm not. There's no reason to believe he did it for me. There's no reason to believe he ever saw me as his fellow. He took no more notice of the man who carried out the whims of his lowest self than he would have of the bootblack who put shine to his shoes.

There have been many times, though, when I've lain sleepless at night harried by the thought that my safety was illusory . . . that perhaps I didn't disappear into the anonymity of the working world, but my whereabouts were known to Jekyll's friends, to be revealed or not as it suited them. Lately, it has come to me that I'd been gulled more than I knew. All those learned treatises about the duality of man and the thin veneer of civilization that appeared after Jekyll's "revelations" came to light, they're all a load of bollocks. I sense Jekyll's hand in this somewhere, his love of deceit and subterfuge. How can we be sure it was his body in that casket borne by grim procession to Highgate Cemetery? London's morgue is full of happy dossers who have shucked off this mortal coil without friend or relation to mourn or identify them. Would it not be like Dr. Henry Jekyll to get another—some unknown, some anonymous roustabout, whose passing has left not a ripple on the surface of the London "that matters"— to take his place on that final journey while he sequesters himself at a friend's country estate or sojourns on the continent? It amazes me that I did not consider this possibility before, but blithely and blindly pursued my rounds of honest toil while Jekyll—my tormentor, my gilded double—remained alive, chuckling to himself at the stupidity of the inferior classes. How easily we are fooled. How unfailingly we accept even the most obvious fictions. How avidly we seize on the story that confirms our prejudice while the unpalatable truth goes begging. Dupes, all of us. And you, too, reader. Wot'cher.

TONY EPRILE's novel, *The Persistence of Memory*, was a *New York Times* Notable Book of the Year and won the Koret Jewish Book prize. His stories—several of which are literary homages—have appeared in *Ploughshares*, *Agni*, *StoryQuarterly*, *Glimmer Train*, *Post Road*, and elsewhere. He teaches fiction in Lesley University's low-residency graduate program.

14

AFTERWARDS

Gregory Maguire

After The Wonderful Wizard of Oz.

WHAT'S THE FIRST THING YOU KNOW IN LIFE? EVEN BEFORE YOU know words? Sun in the sky. Heart of gold in a field of blue, and the world cracks open. You are knowing something. There you are.

As with all of us, the Scarecrow awoke knowing he had *been* for some time already, though unwoken. There was a sense of vanishing splendor in the world about him, an echo of a lost sound even before he knew what *sound* or *echo* meant. The ache of pattern. The backward crush of time and, also, time's forward rush. The knife of light between his eyes. The wound of hollowness behind his forehead. There was motion, sound, color; there was scent, depth, hope. There was already, in the first fifteen seconds, *then* and *now*.

Before him were two fields. One was filled with ripening corn. The other was shorn clean, and grew only a gallows tree in the dead center.

Beyond the fields huddled a low farmhouse, painted blue. And beyond the farmhouse rose a hill, also painted blue, or was that just the color of shadow when the cloud passed over?

A tribe of Crows, black, and thoughtful, sank from a point too high above for the Scarecrow to see or imagine. Their voices brayed insult at him as they fell to the field, ears of green-husked sweetcorn breaking beneath their attack. "Hey there," cried the Scarecrow, "well then!" More instinct than anything else, and not to frighten them away, necessarily. More to announce his notice of them. But they were startled, and wheeled around, and disappeared.

"Who am I?" he said to himself, and then he said it aloud. The sky refused to answer, nor did the corn, the wind, the light—or if they were answering, he couldn't understand the language.

The Crows returned to blot the field before him. With weapons of beak and claw and mighty wing, they beat at the corn, feasting. "Welcome!" called the Scarecrow.

They laughed at him.

One Crow flew nearer. She seemed less interested in the corn than the others. She wore a rhinestone necklace. Her wings were mangy and her eyes, he noticed, rheumy. She was an old Crow and not in the best of health.

"You're supposed to scare us," she said. "Brainless fool."

"Brainless? What do you mean?" he said.

"Think about it. Brainless. No brain."

"How can I think about it if I haven't got a brain?" he wailed.

"You haven't got a brain, haven't got a clue, so you haven't got a chance to keep us from the corn. You're supposed to be *protecting the corn*," she said. Was she being kind, in telling him his life's work, or was she taunting him for being so stupid? She flew nearer, though her cousins were ambushing the ranks of corn with fiercer strength than ever. The Scarecrow had the sense that perhaps she was too old to attack the corn as fiercely as her kin, or perhaps she was too old to be that hungry. Or maybe she just preferred gossip to gluttony.

"Most creatures who can talk can figure out a little," she said. "What's your problem, brother, that you're so dim-witted?"

"My arms hurt. Maybe if they didn't hurt I would be able to think. I need to be able to think. How did I get here?" he said. "At least tell me that."

"Where to start?" she murmured. She stood on a fence rail nearby and settled her head at an angle and looked at him with two black eyes, bright as the backs of beetles. "This is my field, I live here," she said, "I notice what goes on. But where to start?"

"The beginning," begged the Scarecrow.

"A farmer sowed a field not far away, some time ago, and from the seeds he scattered there grew a great lot of hay. Every day he watched the rain water it, and the sun nourish it, and he kept the Cows from tramping it down. It grew up bright as a field of bronzey-green swords. He was proud of that field of hay! And just before the rains at the end of summer, his heart bursting with pride, the farmer swept along the field with a huge scythe, and he cut down the hay to the ground."

The Scarecrow gasped. "He killed it!"

"We call it harvest," said the Crow, "but it looks mighty like killing, I agree. Anyway, the hay lay in fine thick patterns across the field. The farmer picked it up with a fork and loaded it onto a wagon. Later he bound it with twine, and stored the bales in a barn. Most of it he fed to his Cows."

"Cannibals!" snorted the Scarecrow. "He sacrificed his field for the Cows!"

"We call it farming," said the Crow. "And hay cannot talk or think like you and me. But will you pay attention? Sometimes farmers stuff some of their hay into a pair of trousers and a bright red shirt. Then a farmer could put some more into an old farm sack, and paint a face upon it. A farmer could set the sack upon the neck of the shirt, and tie it together with a moldy bit of rope good for little else."

"And then what?" said the Scarecrow.

"Well, that's you," said the Crow.

"Hay and straw and some moldy rope and some second hand clothes? That's all I am?" said the Scarecrow. "The farmer made me? Did he teach me to talk, did he sing me to sleep, did he bless my forehead? But where did the clothes come from?"

"I don't know if the farmer made you," said the Crow, cagily, hiding something. "But he intended to, as he had set aside enough hay for your limbs, and he had chosen the sack and painted your face upon it. And those are his clothes, anyway, so in a sense he is your father."

"Didn't he need them?" asked the Scarecrow.

"No," said the Crow. "Not after a while. Before he could finish you, he fell sick. I suppose he must have died. No man needs his clothes after he's died."

"What does *after* mean?" said the Scarecrow, who was too new to understand befores and afters.

"It means the *next* that follows the *now*, or the *now* that follows the *once*."

"I wish I had a brain," said the Scarecrow. "I understand a man falling sick and dying, but I do not understand befores and afters."

"I saw him through his window, tossing and turning with a fever. It looked bad. I know he must have died, for if he had not, he would be running to berate you for letting us Crows eat all the corn," said the Crow. "But he is dead, and you are all alone. That's too bad, but it can't be helped. I suppose his farmer neighbors took the clothes off his dead body and finished dressing you, and set you on your stake to do the job you were made to do. Too bad you can't do it very well. And now I will stop chatting and go eat some corn myself." Off she flew, in a fluttery, palsied manner, her jewelry flashing in the sun like splashes of fountain. The Scarecrow could see that she had been waiting to peck at ears of corn already cut open by the stronger crows.

"Stop," cried the Scarecrow, "stop!" He did not mean for her to stop eating the corn, for he did not care. He meant to stop her from leaving. But she did not listen.

The Crows made a mess of the cornfield. The Scarecrow knew that the old Crow must have been telling the truth, for no farmer came running from the nearby house to scold him for the damage. But even more damage lay in store. The next day the sky turned hugely purple, and a wind came up from nowhere and flattened the remaining stalks. When the Crows returned, they had to settle their spiky pronged feet in the complicated floor of leaves and stalks, and hunt with lowered heads for what corn could still be found.

"Stop," cried the Scarecrow, "look out! Beware!" But he was not trying to protect the corn. He had seen his friend the Crow, with her collar of fine glints and cold depths, digging deeply for an especially rich ear of corn. Her hearing not what it had once been. From a hump of green rubble launched a missile of red fur and black leather boots, and teeth sharp as the points of rhinestones. Sharper even. The other Crows escaped in an explosion of noisy wings and terrified cries, but the old Crow was too slow. She fell beneath clever paws and hungry jaws, and the jewelry made a bright exclamation mark in the air before it dropped to the ground.

"Yum," said the Fox, after he had finished his meal. "Yes, she was good. But I feel like a little something more." He tried his teeth on the necklace, but it did not appeal to his taste. So the Fox stood up in his black leather boots, and though he could see farther than he would have had the corn not fallen in the wind, he still could not find a suitable sweet morsel to finish his meal. "Strawhead," said the Fox, "you are higher than I. Can you see anything sweet for me to go after?" He licked his chops.

"What do you mean, *after*?" said the Scarecrow, a bit wary, but still curious.

"After?" said the Fox. "*After*? After means *toward*. I go after the Crow, and I get her. I go after my Vixen, and I get her. I go after what I want. What do you want?"

"To understand," said the Scarecrow, sighing.

"Ah, knowledge is sweet, too," said the Fox. He resigned himself to conversation rather than dessert, and he circled himself into a coil of Fox, where he could see how his hind legs ended so magnificently in black leather boots. His bush settled over himself like a blanket. Then he put his chin upon his front paws and looked up at the Scarecrow. His eyes began to close.

"It seems a brutal world," said the Scarecrow.

"Doesn't it though," said the Fox appreciatively.

"You speak as if you know me," said the Scarecrow.

"I believe I know your clothes," said the Fox. "I recognize them. Your clothes make you seem quite familiar. I am happy not to be running from the farmer who used to wear them. When he would see me in his hen-house he would run for a weapon. But now the clothes have survived the man, for he must be dead. Otherwise he would be out here harvesting what is left of his flattened crop of corn. I notice that his clothes are capable of nothing more than housing straw—rather chatty straw, to my surprise, but straw nonetheless."

"He died of a terrible illness, I hear," said the Scarecrow.

"Is that so? Not what I heard." The Fox purred softly at the thought of treachery. "In all likelihood he died over there on the gallows tree. He was to be hung by the neck until he was dead," said the Fox. "The farmer's friendly neighbors intended to break his neck just as I broke the neck of Madame Crow a few minutes ago."

"But why?" said the Scarecrow, alarmed.

"Before you were born, the farmer had gone off to another village to buy some seedcorn, you see," said the Scarecrow, "and when he came back he fell deeply ill. Folks round here are afraid of the plague, and none of them would tend him. He tossed and turned in a raging fever. But somehow he survived, and believed himself to be recovered. He went to the village well and greeted all his neighbors. Within days they succumbed to fevers and fits, and some of them died. The ones who survived blamed him for the outbreak of sickness. They went after him."

"After him," said the Scarecrow, trying hard to understand.

"They said he had caused the death of their loved ones," said the Fox. "They said he had infected them on purpose, so that other families would not have the labor to bring in their corn, and he alone would prosper with a good crop. They came after him with pitchforks and accusations. The farmer was not yet well enough to run away with any speed. They caught him in the middle of the corn. I saw them trap him; I was hiding in the weevily shadows, watching. They went to hang him, much as you are hung there on your stake. I would have stayed to watch the execution, but a sudden summer storm came up, and I fled to my hole. But I suppose they did their job and gave him his death."

"Did he not ask for their charity?" said the Scarecrow.

"Oh, anyone can ask," said the Fox. "No doubt the Crow would have asked for my charity if she'd been able to squeeze breath through her gullet. But charity doesn't satisfy the stomach, does it?"

The Scarecrow didn't know. He tried to close his eyes to squeeze out the sight of the gallows tree in the next field over, but his eyes were painted open. He tried not to listen to the Fox, but his ears were painted open. He tried to still the beating in his chest, but he couldn't; this was because a family of Mice had discovered the Scarecrow and were exploring him as a possible home. It was both uncomfortable and slightly embarrassing to have Mice capering about inside his clothes.

"I suggest you should look for lodging elsewhere," said the Scarecrow in as low a voice as he could manage, "for there is a Fox nearby who likes to go after small creatures."

The Mice took heed and removed themselves to a safer neighborhood. The Fox, nearly asleep, began to laugh softly. "Charity is so appealing in the young," he said, and soon thereafter he began to snore.

The Scarecrow had no choice but to look at the farmhouse, the fields, the gallows tree, the hill beyond them all. The world seemed a bitter place, arranged just so: fields, gallows, house, and hill.

Then around the edge of the hill came a girl and a dog. They were both walking briskly, with a little skip in their step, and from time to time the dog would run ahead and sniff at the seams of the world here and there. The Fox was deep in his dream and the dog would soon be upon him. "Stop!" cried the Scarecrow.

The Fox bolted upright from his sleep and his neck twisted around so his ruff stood out like a brush. He saw the child and the dog, and as the Fox's feet were touching down on the rumpled floor of corn and the scattered black feathers of the Crow, he took just enough time to glance up at the Scarecrow as if to say: Why? Why do you save me, when you disapprove of how I am, when you disapprove of how the world is? Why do you bother?

But he could not take the time to voice the question, for the dog was almost upon him, and the Fox disappeared in a streak of smoke-red against the green-and-gold wreckage of the corn field. He vanished so quickly that he left behind the pair of handsome black leather boots.

The dog barked. It seemed unable to make a sensible remark, and the Scarecrow by now was not inclined to question it anyway. The Scarecrow did not know why he had alerted the Fox to danger. Were the clothes that the Scarecrow was born into the clothes of a kindly man or a terrible one? Who had he been, who was the Scarecrow? What manner of creature, what quality of spirit, what variety of soul?

It was very troubling. The Scarecrow merely watched as the girl approached. By now he did not care to know any more about the world.

The girl wore her hair in pigtails. She was clothed in a sensible dress with an apron tied neatly behind in a bow. She wore neither rhinestones nor black leather boots, but her shoes were glittering in the afternoon sun. "What's that, then?" she said to the dog in a fond voice. "Did you smell something of interest?"

The dog circled about beneath the Scarecrow's pillar, and looked up and barked.

"Why, what do you know," said the girl. "Who are you?"

The Scarecrow didn't know if she was addressing his clothes or his green-gold grasslimbs inside. He did not answer.

"I should like to know which is the best way to proceed," said the girl, almost to herself. "The road divides here, and we could go this way, or that way."

The Scarecrow knew only the house, the fields, the gallows tree, the hill.

"Perhaps it doesn't matter, though," continued the girl, musing. "We didn't choose to come here, after all, so perhaps the choice we make from here doesn't matter."

"What does that mean?" said the Scarecrow.

The girl gave a little start and the dog went and cowered behind the basket she had set down. "I'm a foreigner," she said, "an accidental visitor, and I do not know my way."

"I mean, *after all*," said the Scarecrow. "I do not understand befores and afters. What does *after all* mean? It sounds important."

"After all?" said the girl. She put her head to one side. "It means, when everything is thought about, what you can then conclude."

"If you can't think," said the Scarecrow, "can you have an after all?"

"Of course," said the girl, "but thinking helps."

"I should like to learn to think," said the Scarecrow. "I should like to know about this more, before the world seems too dark to bear."

"Would you like to get down?" said the girl.

This had never occurred to the Scarecrow yet. Well, he wasn't very old. "May I?" he said.

"I will loosen you off your hook if I can reach," said the girl, but she couldn't. Still, she didn't give up. She wandered over across the fields to the farmhouse. The Scarecrow watched her knock on the door, and when there was no answer, he saw her enter. Before long she returned with a little chair. She stood on it and worked at the nail on which the Scarecrow hung. She managed to bend it down, and off he slid, into a heap on the ground.

It felt good to move!

"Whyever did you help me?" he asked.

"Whyever not?" she said, and he didn't know the answer since he didn't know much. But he grinned, for it was fun to be asked, and maybe if she asked him again someday, he would have an answer ready.

"How do you come to be a talking Scarecrow?" she said.

"I don't know," he said. "How do you come to be a talking girl?"

"I'm sure I have no idea," said the girl. "I was born this way."

"So was I," said the Scarecrow. "But my clothes were given me by a dead man, I hear."

He told the girl the story of the farmer who had been treacherously ill, and then had shared his disease with his neighbors, though by chance or intention it could not be said for sure. The Scarecrow told how the neighbors had fallen upon the farmer and killed him for the crime.

The girl looked doubtful. "Who tells you such a grim tale?" she said.

"A Crow, rest her soul, and a Fox, luck preserve him," said the Scarecrow.

The girl looked sadly at the Scarecrow. "You believe everything you're told?" she said.

"I haven't been told a whole lot yet," the Scarecrow admitted. "I'm only two days old, I think."

The girl said, "Wait here while I return the chair to where I found it." And off she went with a thoughtful expression on her face. Her dog followed her with a cheery wag of his tail.

The Scarecrow trusted that she would return. And return she did. She had a calmer look on her face. "The Crow did not know and the Fox did not know," she said warmly. "But I can read, and I do know. I saw a letter on the table in the farmhouse. It was a letter written by the farmer."

"Yes?" said the Scarecrow.

"The letter said, 'Dear neighbors, you will think that I have died. But I have not. When I went over the hill to buy my seedcorn, I fell in love with a woman there. Luck would have it that she felt as fond of me as I did of her. I had hoped to sow my fields and return to marry her, and bring her here, but my sickness prevented my traveling. When you caught me and brought me so close to death on the gallows tree, I thought that was the end. But fate intervened to save me. The storm came up and you all ran for safety. Then appeared my beloved, who had worried that I hadn't returned to her. She had come to find out why, and she had seen you gather, and hid herself in the corn. Seizing her chance, she leaped up and cut me down. So today I am going to marry her. I will not come back to this farm, for I need to make myself a happily ever after somewhere far from here. I have dressed myself in brand new clothes to make her happy with her choice. Here are my old clothes. Please use them for the public good and make a Scarecrow to protect the corn from the Crows. It is your corn now, as it always would have been whenever you needed it. Good-bye.'"

The Scarecrow felt his spirits lift up. "So the owner of these clothes was a man who cared for the well-being of his neighbors, even those who had tried to kill him?"

"I do believe," said the girl, "an unusual man with a good heart."

"We should go tear down that gallows tree in the middle of the next field," said the Scarecrow, "so the neighbors may not try such a scheme again."

The girl peered at it with her hand over her eye. "That is not always a gallows tree," she decided. "It is simply a pole for you to rest upon when that field is ready to be planted with another crop of corn."

The Scarecrow said, "So the stories of the Crow and the Fox were wrong."

"The Crow and the Fox were not wrong," said the girl, "they just did not know what came after." She smiled at the Scarecrow and began to play with bits of corn husk. She made a dolly from an ear of corn, and twisted the leaves of cornstalks to make arms and legs. She dressed it in a rhinestone necklace and a pair of black leather boots.

The Scarecrow waited for the dolly to speak. It was no less than he was, some dead agricultural matter dressed up in human clothes. But it did not speak or move as he did.

"Where was I before I was a Scarecrow?" said the Scarecrow. "Where were you before you were a girl?"

"I do not know that," said the girl, "but I do believe that after you are done being a Scarecrow, and I am done being a girl, we will be something else. You, perhaps, may be a mattress. I will most probably be a woman. We both may be a story that someone else can remember and tell."

"Now?" said the Scarecrow.

"After," said the girl. "But first there's the before, and that's life."

"And what's life?" said the Scarecrow.

"Moving," said the girl. "Moving on. Shall we move on? Will you come with me?"

"Yes," said the Scarecrow. "For the sake of knowing some more about this, of developing my brains so I can treasure this mystery better." Half straw and half human clothes, perhaps, but still hungry for a life to live before so that there could be a story to tell after.

"Which way shall we go?" said the girl.

"Not toward the fields, the house, the hill, the gallows tree," said the Scarecrow. "Let's go in the direction we have not yet gone."

"Good enough for me," said the girl. She left the corn dolly for some other child to find. Then she picked up her basket and the dog came running to her heels. Now that the Scarecrow was down on the ground, he could see that the two fields that made up his world so far were divided by a road paved with yellow brick.

"This way," said the girl. She and the Scarecrow turned their heads toward the west, and began to embroider their befores into a compelling after. For they were searching after, after all, a happily ever after.

GREGORY MAGUIRE is the *New York Times* best-selling author of *Confessions of an Ugly Stepsister*; *Lost*; *Mirror Mirror*; and the Wicked Years, a series that includes *Wicked, Son of a Witch, A Lion Among Men*, and *Out of Oz*. Now a beloved classic, *Wicked* is the basis for a blockbuster Tony Award–winning Broadway musical. Maguire has lectured on art, literature, and culture both at home and abroad. He lives with his family near Boston, Massachusetts.